About the author

Natalia Sheppard is a singer, songwriter, teacher, mentor, inspirational speaker and writer.

She has a B.A. in English Literature, a Diploma in Performing Arts and a Diploma in Teaching, and has spent the last fourteen years touring the globe as a professional singer/MC, working within the Electronic Music Industry. After living in the UK for ten years, Natalia returned to her homeland of New Zealand in 2012, and since then has written and released two albums, one EP, created her own blog and written this, her first novel.

THE LITTLE WHITE HOUSE

Natalia Sheppard

THE LITTLE WHITE HOUSE

Vanguard Press

VANGUARD PAPERBACK

A CIP catalogue record for this title is
available from the British Library.

ISBN 978 1 784653 33 0

Vanguard Press is an imprint of
Pegasus Elliot MacKenzie Publishers Ltd.
www.pegasuspublishers.com

While this story is based on an actual house that existed in rural New
Zealand and many of the events that occurred there, the characters in the
book are fictional. Therefore, any character resemblance to anyone living or
dead is purely coincidental.

First Published in 2018

Vanguard Press
Sheraton House Castle Park
Cambridge England

Dedication

For my mother and father, and my husband, for their support and love, and their endless belief and encouragement while I wrote this book.

Chapter 1

I am not completely sure of the moment when I first realised I 'was', but it must have been not long after I was first created.

There was no 'here I am' moment; more a vague feeling of wakening from a long, dreamy sleep.

I recall feeling the first rays of the morning sun as they hit my corrugated roof, their warm, tender touch growing hot and scorching as the day wore on.

I felt the need to stretch and expand, my body creaking, as the newly milled pine from which I was built popped and loosened in the summer sun's heat.

I took note of myself, from the outside in.

I had been painted white, the smell still fresh and intoxicating on my weatherboard limbs. Several small windows were dotted around my exterior to let the sunlight in, and a chimney was attached to one wall, with a fire inside that would keep my inhabitants and I warm during the winter.

Inside, I was made up of four humble-sized rooms. A small kitchen with linoleum-covered floors and sanded wooden bench surfaces; a sitting room with bare wooden floors; a very small bathroom off the back of the kitchen; and a little bedroom that led straight off the sitting room.

There were hand-woven rag mats on the bedroom floor, scrim covering my walls, and thin cotton curtains hanging in my windows. Everything was simple. There would be no lavish expenses for a little cottage like me.

As I realised I 'was', so I realised I could 'hear' and also 'see'. From this, I learnt I was built to house the farm owner's worker.

Then, there he was. A long, shadowy figure appearing in the sunlight of the open kitchen door, pulling off his gumboots as he stepped inside to inspect me.

He ran a large open palm over my walls and smiled to himself, as he looked from room to room.

"Yeah, this'll do me nicely, Jim!" he called back through the open door.

And then, there was the man who had built me. Striding up to the front step, in two quick movements he removed his boots. He was older than the worker, who was currently inspecting my fireplace. Though his hair was salt-and-pepper coloured and the years working in the wind and rain had drawn deep lines in his face, he was tall and strong, and whistled as he pulled his farm socks back up over his heels.

In that moment, I had a sudden recollection. The whistling, accompanied by a banging sound. The feeling of a breeze rippling through open spaces, the smell of paint and the pulling together of... of... me?

"Yeah, she's not bad, ae?" Jim stepped into the lounge, and immediately I was back in the moment watching, as he gestured towards the kitchen.

"Ya like the curtains the missus has put up for ya? She made those in only a couple of hours!" Jim grinned proudly.

"Yeah, brilliant, mate, it's perfect. Thanks ever so much for sorting me out." The worker held out his open hand with a broad smile and Jim shook it warmly.

"Well, I'll leave ya to move in then. Ya need any more help with the boxes?"

"Nah, she'll be right, mate. I got it from here. See ya tonight for milking."

With that, Jim turned towards the door, tugging on his boots and walking away from me, back towards the main farmhouse, whistling with each stride he took.

As I watched him go, I extended my gaze outwards, past the main house and the huge trees that surrounded it. To my absolute surprise, behind it stood a huge mountain. Tall and pointed at the top, like the roof on the main house, but with a smaller peak echoing its shape, nestled close into its side.

There was a sliver of snow at its summit, but for the most part it looked naked from this far away. I could make out where a bush line began and then ended, and where rock and scoria took over. There wasn't a cloud in the sky, and it was truly one of the most majestic sights I felt I would ever see.

Again, I felt a fleeting moment of recollection. I knew this mountain, I recognised it. It was as if I had looked upon this mountain and the fields surrounding it some time 'before'.

I felt confused. How could I know what it was? In fact, how could I know what anything was, when evidently I was 'brand new'? But I did know. It was as if I had just woken from a long sleep, and was now having trouble deciphering between past and present.

A thump on one of the bedroom floors shook me out of my reverie. I was now watching the worker as he hauled one box after another into my interior.

He pulled in a rickety old wire bed with an overstuffed mattress, which he set down in the bedroom, and haphazardly pulled some sheets and a candlewick bedspread over it.

As he moved around the rooms and became warm with exertion, he opened my windows one by one. I relished the feeling of the summer air drifting through each room, cooling my insides and bringing with it the smell of the nearby hay paddock, mixed in with fresh cow dung.

The worker did not own many things, but with each item he brought in I felt more complete. The clatter of cutlery tipped straight into the drawers, the sheepskin thrown down in front of his chair, even the shotgun laid up behind the front door.

Every little aspect of 'him' became a part of 'me', and I grew more accustomed to him and his habits with each passing day.

I discovered his name was Samuel Watts, but everyone who dropped by tended to call him 'Wattie'. He liked to have a beer each night after milking, and while he was no great chef in the kitchen, he always graciously opened the window so that the smell wouldn't permeate my walls.

He snored in his sleep and sang in the bath, and whenever his clothes needed washing, Jim's wife Meredith would come and collect them to take up to the main house.

From where I sat on the small piece of land opposite the milking shed, I could see most of the day's happenings. Cows being herded in and out at the break of dawn, and again in the evening; Jim and Meredith's children playing in the garden, or them skipping down the track to visit their father. In the mornings I watched as the dray and horses collected huge cans full of fresh milk to take off to the local dairy factory. As the horses moved in unison, their breath coming in snorts of steam, the milk cans would clink softly together, creating their own song.

Often, I would just stare upwards and watch the clouds moving overhead, feeling the warm sunlight bouncing off my roof ridges; sometimes, in the evenings, there would be sunsets that made the entire sky to the west seem alight with fire.

Then would come the evening stars – pinpricks of light on an inky blanket – and I would allow myself to drift away into the darkness, no longer watching or listening to anything at all.

The first time it rained I was taken by surprise, the cold, wet droplets bouncing heavily on my corrugated iron. It was the noise more than the actual temperature of the water that astounded me. But as it rained a few more times, I got used to the experience, and soon I began to enjoy the vibrations and musicality of it.

It was only when the days began to grow shorter, darkness beginning to fall more readily, that I first realised how cold it could be there. The weather seemed to be affected by the close proximity of the mountain, and now each morning it wore a cloak of white snow. Luckily, Samuel loved a warm house, and he got up extra early before milking to light the fire for us. Being such a small cottage, it didn't take long before each room was cosy and warm again, and even though the fire had died down by the time Samuel got back from his day's work, I managed to hold in the heat with what little insulation I had been provided with.

One evening, Samuel came into the house carrying something all wrapped up in his wool coat. He sat down and opened his jacket to reveal a tiny little puppy hiding in there! The puppy was brown and black, with short bristly hair and eyes like little jet-black beads. It squirmed and shook in his arms, whining slightly as Samuel bent down and placed it on the rag mat next to the fire.

"There, there, little one…" Samuel soothed the puppy in a voice I had never heard, one filled with gentle, hushed tones, his hand huge against the little dog's soft, stumpy ears.

"You and me are gonna be great mates, ae? I'll look after ya, don't you worry 'bout that."

Samuel brought in some food from the old truck parked outside, and quickly made a small bed out of an old apple crate lined with some sheepskin scraps.

He put the puppy inside it and watched as it immediately started to gnaw at the edge, its sharp little teeth catching on the wood.

"Don't be wrecking ya bed already... Tess. There's a good girl." I watched enamoured as Samuel tried out the puppy's name. She leapt out of the box and went skittering across the floor, legs skidding on the wooden surface as she ran, so that she landed in a heap.

Samuel gave a joyous, throaty laugh. "Tess, c'mon, get back here!" But the puppy was away, skirting past Samuel's outstretched hands and making him chase her as she gave excited, playful yelps.

This game went on for the next hour, until both were hot and tired from the exertion. Samuel looked at his watch and announced it was time for bed.

Once again he put Tess into her little wooden bed, and this time she stayed.

"Night, night, pup, see you in the morning."

Samuel pulled at the draw-string hanging from the ceiling light in the middle of the room and, as it went out, the room and Tess were bathed in a soft orange glow from the fire.

Samuel threw off his clothes into the corner of his room and pulled on some flannel pyjama bottoms, the bed creaking as he got comfortable.

Within a few minutes, I could hear Samuel's breathing slow as he began to fall asleep, soft and steady, his chest rising and falling, and I waited for his snoring to begin.

In the living room, I could see the puppy's little black eyes peering over the edge of the crate.

She began to whine. Softly at first, but then more urgently, as her fear at being abandoned took over, despite her sleepiness.

In the bedroom, I heard Samuel's heavy breathing stop. He was awake.

"It's all right, Tess pup, I'm here. Go to sleep," he called out, hoping to placate her, but this just made Tess's whining worse. Now she gave little barks that sounded more like a child yelping.

Samuel sighed and swung his legs over the edge of the bed, and stomped sleepily into the living room.

Tess whined louder upon seeing him appear, and she reached her paws up onto the side of the crate, her skinny tail wagging furiously.

Samuel stared down at the puppy, his face softening.

"Oh, come on then, ya poor wee mite." He reached down and pulled the puppy up into his arms. Tess furiously licked at his face in gratitude as he went back into his room and pulled her under the sheets with him. "I suppose it's pretty cold, ae, and we could both do with warming up." Tess snuggled in close to his chest, and within minutes was fast asleep.

Samuel chuckled and kissed the puppy's head, and, moments later, had joined her in a chorus of snoring.

Over the next few weeks they became inseparable, and Tess began to learn the ropes of what it was to be a farm dog, joining him on the farm bike, perched between his legs, as they headed off for the shed.

Every night, even when Samuel insisted on Tess sleeping in her apple crate, she whined until he relented and let her sleep on the bed with him.

When Jim wandered over, he gave Samuel stick over the way he treated her.

"You spoil that dog, Wattie mate! She's s'posed to be a farm dog; that means sleeping outside. Rain or shine!"

"I know, I know, and when it gets warmer I'll get her a nice kennel; but for now, she's still just a young 'un and is missing her mum." Samuel reached down and stroked Tess's head, and she looked up at him with loyal eyes.

Jim shook his head and rolled his eyes.

"Couple of bloody softies," he muttered.

As it was now the depths of winter, the cows went dry, and Samuel no longer had to milk.

I noticed he enjoyed a bit more than his usual one beer before bed, as he sat whittling a piece of wood in front of the fire, or playing tug-of-war with Tess with a piece of old rope.

He fell asleep easily, his snores even louder than before. Still, though, I allowed myself to drift off to the sound of it, until it became nothing more than an echo within my eaves.

The smell of smoke. Strong and choking, and there was something very hot scorching my insides. I felt myself become alert as I scanned first my exterior, and then each room. A fire in the lounge. A spark must have jumped from the fireplace and caught on the rag mat, smouldering at first, then catching on a newspaper nearby on the floor. Now it was crawling up the wallpaper and licking at the curtains. I watched in horror as Samuel stayed in his bed, out for the count and oblivious to what was happening.

Tess, however, sat up, sniffing at the air. She whined slightly and jumped down onto the floor, padding over to look into the living room, where the fire was starting to catch speed.

The heat from the flames was bad. I felt it slice through the scrim on the walls and turn it into dust. Now it was burning into my pine weatherboard, and the lounge window cracked and then shattered with the pressure.

Still Samuel slept on.

Please, I heard myself plead, wake up, get out, and please stop the burning!

I tried to shake off the heat and burning sensation, rattling my roof in terror, the sound of popping as I expanded under the heat.

Tess backed away from the doorway and began to bark. She ran over to the bed and began pawing at Samuel's arm, her body quivering in terror.

Again, I shook and banged my roof, begging and yelling at Samuel to wake.

Suddenly, I heard a shout outside. Jim was running from the main house towards me, his face white with horror. He banged on the door, screaming Samuel's name.

"Wattie! Wattie, get out! FIRE, mate; there's a fucking FIRE!" He threw his body against the door till it gave in and, as he did so, Samuel sat bolt upright in bed, coughing and spluttering. He bounded out of the bedroom door, disorientated and still half asleep, and crashed straight into Jim, who was struggling to see with all the smoke.

"Mate, get out now. Come on!" Jim pulled on Samuel's arm to lead him out, but not before Samuel grabbed Tess by the scruff of her neck.

"Come on, girl!"

Jim, Samuel and Tess burst out of my front door and into the fresh dawn air.

"Quick, get the hose onto her before she's gone!" Jim ordered Samuel. "I'll go get some buckets!"

Samuel, still coughing his lungs out, wasted no time in pulling round the small garden hose which was attached to the wall beside the front door, as Tess cowered under the back of his truck.

He had turned the hose to full, and while it provided some small relief from the burning sensation, the stream of water was not strong enough to fully extinguish the flames that were now threatening to take over my roof.

I was still banging and rattling and carrying on, the heat searing through my structure, which popped and crackled, and I could now feel there was a hole in my wall as the morning air was sucked in by the flames. But then Jim appeared, carrying two large steel buckets − usually reserved for milk − full to the brim with water. He and

Samuel took a side of a bucket each and tossed the water into where the flames were highest.

I heard the fire sizzle and again Jim turned and ran back towards the shed to refill the buckets, while Samuel continued to point the hose at my roof to prevent the flames from going any further.

Then, suddenly, it was all over. The fire was out. The burning sensation still remained slightly, but I no longer felt the immense pain I had a moment ago.

I looked a right mess, with water dripping from my naked beams and wisps of smoke coiling up from piles of black ash. The hole in my wall wasn't as bad as I thought it would be, but I would still need repairing. I noticed the sky was now alight with the grey glow of a chilly winter's dawn.

Jim sat exhausted on the grass, his face filthy with grime. Samuel just stood there in shock.

"M-m-m-mate…," he stammered. "Shit... I nearly... it nearly... Fuck, mate, look at the state of her. I'm so sorry."

"It's all right, mate." Jim got to his feet and threw an arm over Samuel's shoulders. "It must have been the fireplace, ae?" They surveyed my damage.

"It's not too bad; just a bit inside the lounge and this bit of the wall. Don't think it got the roof too bad either... We can fix it. Least you and ya mutt are all right, ae?"

"What the bloody hell happened? Are you lot all right?" a woman's voice exclaimed over their shoulders. It was Meredith, Jim's wife − breathless from running down from the house.

"Nothing too bad, love, just a bit of a fire. I saw it from the toilet window when I got up for a piss!" Jim chuckled.

"Jesus, it doesn't look like it's not too bad – you're lucky you got out, Samuel!" Meredith exclaimed. She came closer. "You boys better come up to the house and get washed up. I'll fix yas some tea."

As they turned and walked away, Jess padding silently at Samuel's heel, I listened as their conversation continued.

"And that noise!" said Meredith. "It woke me from the house! What the hell was it?"

"What noise?" Jim asked her. "We were too busy trying to put the fire out."

"You didn't hear it?" I watched Meredith shake her head. "It was bloody awful, really loud, like someone was screaming."

Chapter 2

I sat idle for a couple of days shivering in the freezing winter cold, my living room exposed to the elements due to the gap in the wall, while Jim ordered some replacement wood.

Luckily, it only rained once, a light rain that washed some of the soot and rubble away, turning it into a black stream that trickled out onto the grass.

Samuel used a huge wooden broom with thick wire bristles, and swept out all the remaining debris.

The two of them, plus one of Jim's brothers, boarded up my gaping wall with new pieces of pine, and reinsulated me with scrim, before covering it over with a new piece of internal board.

Meredith came with a couple of new mats she had ragged, and then they painted the whole of my living room's front wall white.

While the singed floorboards' black colour did not match the others, and the painted wall did not match the walls throughout the rest of my interior, I did not mind. Even the windows being open in the chilly air to let the paint dry did not bother me. I felt grateful I had been saved, that Samuel had been saved, that I was even being repaired.

This time, though, Samuel would not live in me.

As they mended and painted and repaired, and Tess sat watching in the corner, I heard the conversations that went back and forth. Samuel was leaving to go and work on a bigger farm, and Jim was going to sell me on to someone else. He and Meredith needed to save some money, and soon Jim's son would be able to help him with the farm.

I felt afraid. I liked being here on the farm with the milking shed, the mountain and the trees. I liked being able to see the main house and I liked belonging to Jim and Meredith, and having Samuel and Tess live within my rooms.

Where would I go? HOW would I go?

But the day eventually came, and Samuel put all his things back into boxes and dragged the rickety wire bed back out through my front door.

Tess danced excitedly outside, barking and wagging her tail with anticipation as the last of Samuel's things were loaded onto a trailer attached to his truck.

"See ya, ol' girl!" His voice echoed throughout my empty rooms. "You've been good to me!"

And with that, he slammed the door, revved the engine, and was down the farm track, leaving a cloud of dust in his wake.

I sighed into my foundations and waited.

For a few weeks I sat there, nothing happening. A soft snow fell one night and covered my roof and front step. I heard Jim and Meredith's now-teenage children come running out of the main house, whooping and laughing. But they did not come down to see me.

I watched as the cows were moved closer to the shed once more and heard the sound of baby calves being born in the night, as Jim and his son walked amongst them with a torch, helping where they could.

I felt the sunlight become warmer and the shadows grow longer, as daffodils sprang up around my grass where the fire had once scorched it to its roots, their yellow mouths hanging open, declaring a fanfare for spring.

And still I waited.

Then one day a man came and disconnected the wires that had stretched from the front of my eaves to the lichen-covered power pole alongside the track.

Then another man came and disconnected all the pipes that had held my plumbing in place.

Then Jim, and his brother and one of the neighbours from across the main road, came with shovels and dug all around my walls and foundations.

A huge long chain was wrapped around my exterior and attached to a harness.

Finally, a team of men came and I was slowly raised upwards using stumping jacks. Two huge logs were slid under my floor joists to support the weight, and then, at the top of these logs, were positioned a group of smaller, thinner logs that the bigger logs would be rolled up and onto.

Then the harness was attached to a group of Clydesdale horses, who slowly pulled the logs until they began to move. As I rolled forward, the group of men, including Jim, raced around the back, taking the smaller logs from there and bringing them around to the front so I could creep further onwards. I became excited now. I was moving! I was going somewhere! I could see right down the track to the main road now, where every now and then a car or truck would rattle by.

I could see the neighbour's house and garden, and their cows in the paddocks further beyond.

There were a lot of people there watching and helping as I was moved slowly down the track. Jim and his family, plenty of the neighbours, and even some passing cars had pulled over to the side of the road to observe as I neared the end of the track.

"Goodbye!" I wanted to call out. "Goodbye, Jim!" I felt both sad and scared, but excited and full of anticipation.

The horses turned right onto the main road and now moved slowly Westwards.

The road – 'Eltham Road' – was straight as an arrow in either direction. In the far distance to the West I could make out the horizon, a thin line defining the sky and... a shimmering blue line of a different hue. But what was it?

Before I could decide, I felt the horses slow. We had barely gone a few miles down the road and we were already slowing to a stop. There to the left of us was a gap in the hedge. A small plot of land was waiting, with foundations ready for me to fit onto. I couldn't believe it! I was only moving down and across the road!

And there was Jim and the neighbours still watching and waiting as I was freed from the horses and harness of chain, and rolled off the logs amid lots of yelling and pointing. I felt happy enough. I wasn't going far. I could even see the mountain above the hedge still!

I took it all in as my structure was fitted into place, and my electrics and plumbing were connected. I sat facing the Eltham Road, but just back from it, surrounded by the beginnings of a hedge, with space for a garden. To the right of me were paddocks, and to the left of me another small paddock which led onto a river. Across the river was a bigger house and back behind that a milking shed.

I looked outwards at all the people who were standing there watching and chatting animatedly, and I wondered who it was I would belong to now.

In the months that followed I met the people who owned me, but who would not live in me. Again, I was to house farm workers who would help with the milking and maintenance of the farm where I sat.

But firstly the farm owners, Jack and Ruth Barry, set about making me fit to house a family. Their workers had children!

The first thing they did was add a wash-house onto my back part, and give me a back door which was made of solid rimu wood.

The wash-house had bare wooden floors, and Jack bought in two concrete tubs and a mangle wringer washing machine that was heavy and required help in moving. (It also shook me to my very foundations whenever it was used!)

Off the bedroom to the right, another bedroom was added, and, at the front of my structure, a small 'sun room' was built on.

My kitchen was given a new 'Zip' boiler, which, when you pulled a string, heated up the water instantly; and Jack and Ruth laid a simple carpet throughout my living room and new bedrooms. I felt myself swell with pride as these new rooms were added. Though at times I was uncomfortable while parts of me were knocked through, and it took a bit to adjust to my new additions, I was getting bigger! (Although I was still only a tiny cottage compared to the houses I saw around me.)

I was so excited to meet my new inhabitants, and when they finally arrived – a family of five – they did so in a cacophony of shouting, slamming, crying, laughing and heave ho-ing of boxes and furniture.

I tried to take everyone in all at once, but the children kept running in and out of my new back door and in circles round and round my outsides.

This family had a different way of speaking to what I was used to hearing, and I soon discovered this was because they did not come from here, but another place far away called England. The children, two girls and a boy, were aged six, eight and ten. Their parents were called Charlie and Ethel, and this was not the first farm they had worked on since coming to New Zealand.

They were a noisy family, often talking in loud voices, and one of the girls was prone to screaming: whether in delight or fear, anger or fright, it didn't matter.

I wasn't used to such a hubbub and it took me a few months to get used to them all.

However, they were a lovely lot, who seemed to get along well enough, and enjoyed being together.

Ethel had lots of black and white photos which she had stacked up on top of a side table, and a wireless radio took pride of place on another table next to the fireplace.

At night, the family would gather around the wireless and listen to talking or music. This was my first time hearing music that wasn't coming out of Samuel's mouth from in the bath. It was amazing! I got to know all the songs that were played regularly, two of the favourites being 'Great Balls Of Fire' and 'Peggy Sue', which went down well in the house as one of the girls' names was Susan.

As the days became warmer, I relished having that extra back door. The cool summer breeze would float in through it and out of the open windows at my front. I stretched as much as I could in the heat, trying to give myself room, my roof rattling as I did so; but one night, when the girls were talking in the bedroom they shared, I heard one of them whisper to the other, "The noises the house makes, especially at night, are scary. All that creaking and groaning. I don't like it." So I tried not to do it as much, at least not when there was someone at home

However, I was rarely alone. There was always comings and goings of some sort; Charlie off to the shed, Ethel taking the kids to school in their battered Austin A55, people calling in for cups of tea. The children were obviously popular at their local school, with a stream of friends in to play each weekend.

One hot sunny Saturday, Charlie announced they were all going to 'the beach'.

I had never heard of the beach, and listened intently as the children flapped about the house excitedly, the young boy, John, bragging about how he was going to swim as far out as his sisters, Susan lamenting that she needed a new suit, and the other sister, Kitty, screaming as per usual over how amazing it was all going to be.

"For goodness sake, would you stop screaming, Kitty? And Susan, we cannot afford to get you a new swimsuit, so for now just put your other suit on and stop going on at me!"

The family eventually managed to get themselves together, lunch in brown paper bags, towels and togs in the boot of the car, doors slammed, including my own, and they were off with a puff and wheeze from the car, and out along the road.

Silence.

It felt unusual to be so alone and for things to be quiet for a change. I took note of the flowers that Ethel had planted in their small garden outside my wash-house door, and the vegetables that were sprouting in the sunshine. I listened as the birds sang in the hedge which was growing at a very fast pace, and heard calves in the nearby paddock mooing to each other, their days spent frolicking in the grass, or sheltering from the sun and rain under the hedges.

I looked at the huge trees in the distance, the tops of their heads bowing slightly in the wind. Again, I had a moment where I felt a familiarity with the scene, but from a different perspective.

It was as if I had always been here in this place – 'Awatuna', I had heard Ethel and Charlie call it one day – yet I knew I had not always been here as I was now.

In the beginning I used to be confused by these visions and thoughts, but now I was starting to grow accustomed to them. I knew I had been 'built'. I had heard both Jim and Charlie talk about this. I knew my structure was made from 'pine' wood, and that wood came from trees. So was I a tree before this? Or many trees?

Did I think and feel the same in the 'before' time?

These thoughts usually petered out eventually because either I grew tired with my own questions, or, as with now, the family would come home and my attention would be turned back to the present moment.

Charlie, Ethel and the children were exhausted but exhilarated after their day at the beach. I bathed in their happy recollections of swimming in the 'sea', building sand castles, and even a treat to the ice cream shop. The beach sounded like an amazing place.

That night, as they all sat round their 'Formica' dining table eating their mince and vegetables, Charlie and Ethel told the family they had an announcement.

"Okay, everyone, things are going to get a little cosier around here in a few months' time," Charlie began; "Mum is going to have another baby." He pointed towards Ethel's stomach. "So everyone needs to start helping out a bit more too."

Kitty screamed in delight, and Susan and John started chattering away excitedly, as Ethel sat there, smiling serenely.

A Baby! I trembled in excitement and my front door bumped on its hinges. I had never had a baby within my walls before! This certainly was an exciting day!

Over the next few months, as Ethel grew larger with her impending birth, she brought out baby clothes that had been stored in boxes under the bed, and washed and aired them on the wire washing line strung between the house and the hedge. A wicker Moses basket − "The same one you slept in," Ethel told the children − was lovingly made up with hand-knitted woollen blankets.

The evenings' summer warmth was now long gone and was instead replaced by a bitter breeze that seemed to come straight off the mountain and in under my roof, chilling me until Charlie got the fire going.

Then, one late autumn afternoon, as Ethel was standing at the kitchen bench peeling carrots, I saw her face wince with pain and she gripped the side of the sink so hard her knuckles turned white.

Charlie was at the shed bringing the cows into milk, Kitty was at a friend's and Susan was outside chopping some kindling for the fire which they had begun lighting that week as the weather got cooler. Only John, who was at the table doing school work, heard his mother's small gasp.

"You alright, Mum?"

"The baby!" Ethel whispered through clenched teeth. "It's… coming... and it's coming early!"

"What... now?" John jumped up from the table and rushed to Ethel's side.

He helped her over to the armchair that their Father usually sat in to read his paper.

"Get Susan!" Ethel ordered. "Tell her to go and fetch your Father... and to hurry!"

Ethel looked down the dampness that was now spreading across the front of her dress.

John rushed outside and relayed the information to Susan, who dashed off out the front gate and up the road to the next driveway.

Ethel groaned some more and clutched at her stomach, and this time John helped her into the bedroom, where she lay down, panting in small, sharp breaths.

After what seemed like forever, Susan came running back in, this time with the farm owner's wife, Ruth.

"Ethel!" she called, moving swiftly into the bedroom. "Ethel, are you all right?"

"Ruth! The baby is coming! Where is Charlie? He needs to drive me to the hospital!"

"Gary said he's over the back; one of the cows hurt her leg on the way up the race! But I can take you!" Ruth reached out and tried to help Ethel up off the bed.

"Argh! No.... no, I don't think we have time!" Ethel fell back against the bed. This time she gave a roar that rattled my window panes. "It's coming now!" Ethel cried.

The look on Ruth's face turned from fear, to panic, to sudden determination.

"Righto then, love, if it's coming now, let's sort you out." Ruth turned to Susan and John, who were standing in the bedroom doorway, a look of fear on both their faces.

"John, darling, you go up to our house and you stay there, OK? You don't come back until someone comes and gets you, all right?" John nodded nervously, but did as he was told, dashing back out my front door and up the road.

"Susan, you're gonna have to be a big girl now and help me and your Mum, all right?"

Susan swallowed hard and looked at her mother, who was now red-faced and panting faster. Ethel nodded at Susan. "You can do it, darling."

Then there was a flurry of action. Susan and Ruth grabbed towels and as much linen as they had, plus hot flannels and the sharpest knife in the kitchen drawer.

Outside, the sky grew dark and a wind got up. The washing on the line danced in jerking movements with every gust.

I was terrified by Ethel's cries. I rattled my windows and doors on their hinges with every anticipated scream. It seemed to go on forever, although later I learned it was only about twenty minutes! The rain outside started to lash down, beating at my windows, as Ethel pushed and moaned, a low and desperate sound that I had never heard before.

And then, in a final push, Ethel gave birth to her little boy.

His body was tiny and lifeless as Ruth used the kitchen knife to cut the cord binding him to his mother. She rubbed his face and body gently with a towel and handed him to Ethel, but the little body made no sound. His skin looked ashen and loose.

"What's happened?" Susan whispered in fear. "Why is he not crying? Why isn't he moving?"

Ethel broke down in tears. "Oh no... Oh no... He's too small. He.... he's just too small."

She clutched the baby to her chest and softly sobbed.

Ruth wiped her eyes, tears mixed with sweat running down her face.

"I'm so sorry, Ethel." She reached out to tenderly touch her shoulder.

For a moment their cries were drowned out by the sound of the wind which was now howling in and around my window panes, and getting in under the gaps between my walls and the roof.

I wanted the wind to stop so they could be in peace. I felt responsible for the eerie noise that filled the room, whistling and wailing as if in mutual sadness.

And then I heard Ethel gasp. "Wait!... He's... he's breathing!" Ethel looked down at the little baby whose tiny chest was indeed moving up and down, if only slightly.

She opened her blouse and pulled down her bra, holding the baby against her hot, flushed skin.

"Keep him to your chest!" Ruth replied, running out of the room. "Keep rubbing his back!"

She returned with a couple of towels that had been warming by the fire and wrapped them around both Ethel and the baby. Ruth and Susan pulled the blankets up around Ethel's chest, as she continued to rub her baby's tiny fragile frame and whisper encouraging words. The baby gave the tiniest of squawks, but for the most part was quiet as he filled his lungs with each desperate breath.

And still the wind howled.

As the baby's breathing steadied, Ethel gave him to Susan to hold while she gave birth to the placenta. Then he was straight back onto his mother's bare chest to keep him as warm as possible.

Ruth ran out and got the washing in as the clouds continued to release their pent-up fury, and then busied herself in the kitchen, fixing the tea and keeping the fire roaring. Susan was sent out in the rain up to the milking shed to tell her father the news, and to collect John, who had been waiting anxiously at the main house.

By the time Kitty got home from her friend's, and Charlie was back from milking, the baby had begun to suckle Ethel's breast. Despite the storm that was carrying on outside, inside the chaos from before had calmed to a warm, cosy quiet.

Ruth offered to look after the children, as Charlie had to drive Ethel to the local hospital in Kaponga so they could be checked over.

"Thank you so much for everything." Ethel smiled up at her. "I think we will call him Barry – after you and Jack."

Ruth looked delighted. "I can't wait to tell Jack! Now off you go. I will look after the children."

I felt a tremendous relief that everything within my wooden walls was now calm.

Despite the wind and the rain outside, I felt proud that I could keep this family safe and warm. I had been built well. I might be just a little white cottage, but I was all this family had right now, and it was enough.

Early the next morning, just after milking, Charlie arrived back home on his own and explained to Ruth and the children that Ethel and baby Barry would have to stay at Kaponga Maternity Hospital, where Ethel would rest for two weeks, and Barry would be monitored.

That evening, just before dinner, Ruth came back to the house, and this time she had a strange lady with her.

Ruth gathered the children and Charlie into the lounge.

"Everyone, this is Mere Kahui. She is from the Women's Division and will be doing the cooking and cleaning and that while ya Mum is in the hospital. You listen to her and do what she says when ya Dad's not here, all right?"

The children nodded solemnly at the strange lady standing there, holding a crochet travel bag in her hands. She was tall and serious and looked the children over one by one.

"I guess you can have our room," Charlie mumbled, his usual cheery self suddenly meek and tired. "I'll sleep in here on the sofa."

Over the following two weeks, Mere did indeed do the cooking and cleaning, but she also made sure the children did their homework, helped with the chores and would hear no word of an argument.

Any time one of the children protested at anything Mere asked them to do, she would knit her eyebrows together in a furious frown, purse her lips, and, with hands on her enormous hips, would stare them down.

"You don't talk back to your elders, ae! You do as you're told, ae; and if you don't, I'll get that jam spoon round your back legs!"

By the time Ethel and baby Barry returned from the hospital healthy and well rested, the children and Charlie were so excited to have them home. They couldn't wait to be rid of Mere, or 'The Battle Axe', as they all called her behind her back. However, no one could deny that she had certainly kept a tight ship while Ethel had been away.

Barry was a cheerful little boy who grew into his personality more and more, although he was always small for his age. Over the next few years he was often ill with chesty coughs and could never run or play for more than a short amount of time before he became breathless and tired, but this did not get him down. He had been told from an early age that he was lucky to be alive, and so he made the most of every day. Ethel tried not to baby him, but I knew she couldn't help but feel worried whenever he went out with the others to play.

In the meantime, Jack and Charlie built a car shed to house the Austin, and Susan started high school in the local town of Opunake to the West.

An old rumbling bus drove all around the area collecting school children who stood outside their houses waiting for their pick-up. One afternoon, when Susan came home from school, she and Kitty got into a furious argument.

"I cannot share a room with her any more, Mum!" Susan came stomping into the tiny kitchen. "She gets into all my things; I have no privacy; the house isn't even big enough to have friends over!"

John, who had been sitting in the corner reading a book, rolled his eyes.

"You think *you* don't have enough space! What about me, having to share with a toddler in a room the size of a cupboard!" He indicated towards the sun room, which housed two single beds practically side by side.

"I know, I know!" Ethel sighed, throwing the damp dish-cloth in her hand into the sink.

"I've spoken to your Father about this. He enjoys working for Jack and Ruth, though."

"Well, tell them to build us a bigger house!" Susan retorted, throwing her hands up in the air in frustration. "I hate living here!"

She flounced out of the room and into the bathroom, slamming the door behind her.

For the first time in my being, I felt hurt. It was hard to hear that the family was growing frustrated by my size. When the children were younger, I had been the perfect space for them to enjoy; but I now sensed that this was about to change.

And I was right. Over the next month, Charlie and Ethel discussed the pros and cons of leaving, and eventually it was decided that Charlie would look for work elsewhere, on a farm with a bigger worker house for them, and perhaps closer to Opunake for the children to go to High School. When Charlie found another farm job, all the children could talk about was how much fun they were going to have in their new, bigger house.

I felt my eaves sagging as the family packed up around me. The black and white pictures were taken down, the wireless placed carefully into a box stuffed with newspaper. It took about a week for everything to be ready and loaded into the Austin; and, after about three trips back and forth to the new farm, Charlie came back and collected Ethel, Susan, Kitty, John and Barry for the last time.

The children sat in the back of the car ready and waiting, but Ethel hung back, walking through my empty rooms, taking it all in. She stood silently at the door to their bedroom, looking at the space where their bed had been. Then, without another word, she turned on her heels and left, closing my front door quietly behind her.

Chapter 3

I was alone again, but not for long, and for that I was grateful. Jack hired another worker, Gary Turner and his wife Irene, and they arrived with seven children in tow.

Before the family made the move, Jack and Gary built a sleep-out onto the back of the car shed. In this they built bunk beds for three of their eldest boys, while back inside my walls, their other three boys shared one of the rooms, and their only daughter had the sun room. Jack also ran a power line from the front of my roof to the sleep-out so the boys could have lights and a small bar heater.

Over the next year and a half, I only had snatches of silence within my walls. Even at night, there was the sound of heavy breathing, snoring, sometimes tears from nightmares, secret whispered conversations across the room, and so forth.

They furnished me very simply, and while no one was especially messy, it was hard to keep a house of nine people clean.

All of the children had chores both at home and on the farm, which kept a steady stream of people moving in and out of my doors, but there were times when everyone could be in the lounge at once. There were play fights that often escalated quickly, and tables were overturned, books knocked off shelves and one of my internal walls had a perfectly round hole in it from a mis-thrown punch.

Irene tried to control them all as much as she could, but she was often away from the house helping Gary with the farm, especially during calving season, so the children looked after each other.

During this time, a possum made its way up one of the drainpipes, wiggled underneath my eaves and made a nest in between my roof and the ceiling.

In the day, when it was hot, the possum slept, but at night it would scuttle around on the ceiling boards, and climb out onto my roof in the cool night air, running back and forth.

Some of the family would wake and there would be shouting and the banging of broomsticks on the ceiling, threats to 'Shoot the bloody bastard', and even a night when Gary ran outside in his pyjamas and threw a brick at the escaping possum! The brick missed the possum completely, but landed with a dull thud on my corrugated roof, where it sat for the next two years.

The wash-house was always full of gumboots and overalls hung up on the wooden pegs that were stuck in the wall, and dinner time was a fight to the death over who would get the last bit of meat. Even Gary didn't stand a chance against his hungry brood.

Clothes were shared between siblings, and the mad dash for the school bus in the mornings always meant something was left behind.

My walls were scuffed and doorways chipped, and the light in the lounge had its pull cord tugged so hard it broke off half way, so none of the shorter children could reach to turn it on, other than jumping up and down several times. The carpet in the lounge had a path of lighter-coloured weave, where a constant tread of feet from kitchen through to the bedrooms wore it down.

Sometimes on a Saturday night, Gary would go to the local pub and a couple of hours later his Ford Anglia would come roaring into the drive and towards the car shed at such speed I feared he may go straight through the back and into the sleep-out. Despite Irene's protests at him to 'Shut the bloody hell up', he would always come dancing into the house singing 'What's New, Pussycat?' or some other pop tune at the top of his voice.

One night he came in singing as usual and this time grabbed Irene up from her chair and, much to the kids' delight (and more of Irene's protests), danced her around the lounge as she struggled against his arms. Suddenly, Gary broke into 'I Can't Get No Satisfaction' and rolled his eyes at the kids, who by then were in stitches, giggling on the floor. At that, Irene gave him a shove in mock disgust and stalked off into the bedroom. Gary gave his kids a wink and followed his wife into the bedroom, where they then heard their Father begging his wife for a kiss, followed by a couple of sharp words from their Mum, and then the sound of bumps, rustling bedclothes and bed springs squeaking.

About ten minutes later, the children heard their Father's snores, and Irene came back into the lounge adjusting her dishevelled hair and smoothing down the front of her dress. She glanced down at her giggling children.

"All right then, you lot, everyone off to bed!" She clapped her hands at her kids, who sprang up from the floor and headed off to fight for room in the bathroom.

I watched Irene as she looked around her, surveying the usual mess scattered across the lounge floor. She sighed and shook her head as she murmured to herself, "This just will not do."

I knew then that the Turner family would not be staying much longer.

After they eventually left, I sat empty for some time. I am not exactly sure why, or for how long, but no one came to see me, other than Jack, who walked through my rooms shaking his head at the scruffy state of me.

"Sorry, mate," he said, looking at the wall where some of my wallpaper had begun to peel, "ain't got any money to fix ya right now; got other priorities."

His footsteps echoed through the rooms and out the front door, where he locked it behind him and began walking up the path.

I felt tired and sad. I sighed into my foundations, the weight of my walls creaking against the floorboards.

Outside, Jack stopped in his tracks, and turned from the road back to face me. He shaded his eyes and looked hard at me. "What'd you say?"

There was a pause, as if he was waiting for an answer. Jack looked baffled for a minute, before he shook his head and broke into a smile.

"Going fuckin' barmy, I am!" He laughed at himself again and turned and walked off down the road.

Days passed in a sort of sleepy haze. Dust danced in the sunlight which filtered in through my closed windows. The possum left her nest for more comfortable climes, and a family of starlings moved into the eaves instead.

The wall where my paper peeled cracked some more, until a large strip hung down, almost grazing the floor, and my 'Pinex' ceiling began to sag.

But I didn't feel too lonely. I needed the rest. After years of continuous noise from two big families, I had almost forgotten what silence felt like, and it was never too quiet anyway.

The starlings sang and chatted away, the paddock right next to me was often full of cows, and sometimes in the distance I would see Jack feeding out on his tractor, or could just make out Ruth up at the big house hanging out her washing. Cars continued to race past on the Eltham Road, and huge milk trucks now began roaring up and down it.

Then, one spring day, when I was in one of my hazy warm dazes, I heard a car pull up in the driveway. A young couple climbed out, huge smiles on their faces, and walked up and unlocked my front door. They walked through my rooms, taking me in, making comments about my appearance and occasionally giggling excitedly.

Their names were Joan and David, and they would be my next inhabitants.

Joan and David were nineteen and twenty-one and were newlyweds. They also owned barely a thing in the world.

Over the years, both Charlie and Ethel and the Turner family had painted various parts of my internal walls here and there where needed, but instead of looking fresh and new, I had just looked more haphazard as time went on, as the tone of colour never seemed to be the same.

The layers of paint had built up in some parts, leaving sections of the wall thicker than others, but Joan and David didn't have the time or money to strip back all the paint. Instead, they pulled off the peeling wallpaper, wiped my walls down, and then applied one coat of off-white throughout each room. At least I looked consistent for a change!

Joan swept out all the cobwebs, vacuumed my threadbare carpet, cleaned my windows and scrubbed down my Formica surfaces. The claw-foot bath was stained from a leaky tap, but she still managed to give it a good clean with some baking soda, vinegar and a steel-wool cloth.

Outside, my paint job was no better, so David set to scrubbing my outsides down, before giving me a couple of layers of white house paint. I had not looked this good in years, and I swelled slightly in pride, my pine limbs stretching outwards towards the garden and car shed.

Joan and David collected whatever they could to furnish me. Some sofa squabs that used to be in an old caravan were placed on top of large apple boxes, and once they were covered with the tartan rugs that David had gotten for his twenty-first birthday, they seemed to make rather comfortable seating.

Their bed was a hand-me-down from an older brother, and Ruth had loaned them an old oak wardrobe from the big house in which Joan kept her two best (and only) dresses.

In the corner of the lounge, in pride of place, was Joan's surfboard. This, I learned, was another thing used at 'the beach', as I watched her race off with it in the car one day, and come back a few hours later, her hair wet and matted, skin pink from the sun, and a huge smile on her face.

I was embarrassed by my Pinex ceiling as it was drooping in places, but David hammered in nails to try to keep it up as best he could. I began to feel more and more receptive to Joan and David and the energy they brought into my rooms. While there were some things that could not be changed, such as my worn-out carpet, the two of them made a home out of what they had and what they could.

Joan sewed bits of old thick blankets together and lay them down over the mismatched carpet near the fireplace. David decided the garden needed more than just a barberry hedge, and over a weekend made a little wooden picket fence that he painted white to match. The fence was erected at the front in place of some of the hedge which was pulled out, put into a pile in the paddock next door and burned.

It turned out that Joan was an aspiring artist who painted oil paintings of the local scenery. She asked

David to hammer in some hooks and, for the first time ever, my walls were covered with art.

Ruth and Jack popped in to make sure everything was all right, and were genuinely taken aback by what they saw.

"Goodness!" exclaimed Ruth. "I can't believe what you have done with the place. It's so much tidier and homely than it's ever been. You even have real paintings on the walls!"

Joan blushed with pleasure at the compliment as she pulled the zip cord to boil some water. "Thanks so much, Ruth," she replied. "It is such a lovely little house really." This time it was I who felt pleased, my corrugated roof creaking in happiness.

"Bit noisy, though!" said David. "It makes a hell of a noise at times, creaking and groaning like that." He pointed upwards to my roof.

"Yeah, I know, mate," Jack nodded. "Sometimes it sounds like it's bloody alive!" He laughed loudly, shaking his head incredulously at the thought.

"Well then, you had best treat the house with care, and it will be good to you in return," Ruth replied. She got up and walked into the kitchen to help Joan make the tea.

David and Jack began discussing the arrangement of Joan and David living there. It transpired that the reason I had sat unkempt for so long was that Jack and Ruth were building a bigger house for themselves and that the current main house would soon become the new place for their share milkers to live.

I was deemed just too small for families to keep inhabiting, so it made sense for them to rent me out to a couple.

In the meantime, David's parents lived further up the road in a home that was currently being updated. When it was finished, his parents were to move to the city, and David and Joan and their future children would take over the farm and that house. So, I was to be just a temporary home for David and Joan, which was rather disappointing, as I enjoyed their company and how well they looked after me.

"So the rent is $20 a week, which you can just pay me in cash if ya like," Jack explained. "Ya Dad said the house should be ready for you in about six months, so I'll arrange someone else to come in after you move up the road."

"Sounds good to me." David smiled, extending a hand. The two men shook on it. "And, ah... while ya here, we may as well tell ya the... ah... news."

He called for Joan and Ruth to join them in the lounge.

"Thought we should tell them the news," he said, looking at his young wife.

"Go on then," Joan replied, suddenly looking like she wanted to be anywhere at that moment but in the lounge with her landlords.

"Joanie's pregnant," David announced. "But we don't really want the neighbours to know at this stage, as ah... as ah...," he stammered and blushed as the words failed to form.

"We got pregnant before we were married," Joan finished the sentence for him, her cheeks blazing with embarrassment. "That's why we had to get married so quickly after the engagement." They both looked at Ruth and Jack, expectantly awaiting their response.

But all Ruth could think to say was, "But Joanie, you went surfing two days ago!"

Joan laughed. "I know, I know. I'm only three months, though, and I just thought I'd get one more day in..." She trailed off, looking even more embarrassed, as she realised how silly her words sounded.

"Well... congratulations, mate, that's brilliant," Jack broke the silence and reached out to shake David's hand again.

"Yes, yes, congratulations!" Ruth pulled Joan in for a hug. "And don't worry, no one will know the situation. By the time you're nearly due, you'll be up at the big homestead anyway, and running the farm. That's all anyone will care about!" She gave Joan an understanding smile, and the uncomfortableness that had permeated the room a minute ago was gone.

Chapter 4

David worked most days for his father, while Joan kept the house tidy, and knitted clothes for the baby. Every now and then, she would stop and stare at her surfboard and give a big sigh. I knew she was dying to take it to the beach, but as her belly was now starting to swell, it was out of the question.

As well as her surfboard, Joan loved her music. They had a radio that David's Dad had lent them, which Joan turned up to full volume whenever she was home on her own. Her favourite songs were 'I Wanna Hold Your Hand' by The Beatles and 'A World Of Our Own' by The Seekers. Joan would sing at the top of her voice and dance around the room, even at five months pregnant.

Sometimes she just sat in the sun and talked to her unborn baby. She told the baby, and, inadvertently, me, the story of how she and David had met at High School. How he had been charming and funny, and while Joan wasn't sure she liked him at first, he won her over with his wit and lust for life, and his obvious lust for her!

I liked these moments of stillness and quiet, Joan's soft husky voice, the occasional car hurtling past on the road, and me: the little white house on the side of the road, within whose walls a young woman lay, with life growing inside her own belly's walls.

One autumn afternoon, Joan was stretched out on the lounge floor in the thinning afternoon sunlight. She had pulled her top up so her rounded stomach was exposed, basking in the warmth, her eyes partially closed.

I was dozing with her, enjoying our solitude, when I felt a rumble far beneath my foundations. At first I thought it was probably just a milk truck coming at speed down the road, especially when I heard the growling noise that was moving with it. Suddenly, however, the rumble seemed to hit full force at the earth underneath me, and without warning I felt myself being jolted from side to side with a violence I had never known.

Joan's eyes shot open and she gave a gasp as she pulled herself to her feet.

"Oh God, oh God, oh God!" she cried, her eyes darting round the room for somewhere to go. The paintings on my walls bounced up and down, and the plates in the cupboards rattled right out of their shelves, crashing into smithereens on the floor. Joan struggled to stand upright as she staggered like a drunk from side to side towards the front door. I tried to clutch onto my foundations as best I could, but the old bricks on my chimney cracked and swayed for a moment, and then, in an almighty THUMP, the top half toppled and fell onto the grass outside, bringing ash and dust down the chimney and into the lounge in a gushing black cloud.

Then, as quickly as it hit, the shaking stopped. The rumbling moved onwards through the ground like a savage animal on the prowl.

I was rattled all over. My pine limbs had weakened in the shake, and the bedroom door hung slightly at an angle where my floor had dropped.

Joan stood at the front door, dazed. She held tight to the door frame and exhaled. "Bloody hell!" she exclaimed to herself. "A bloody earthquake!... That was a fucking bloody earthquake!" And with that, she started to laugh almost in disbelief. She looked around her at the mess of broken plates and the ash cloud that was filling the room and laughed some more. "Blimmin' heck, I can't believe it, that was a pretty big one!" She let go of the door frame and wiped her face. I could see the pulse in her neck beating fast with the shock and excitement of it all.

Within a few minutes, David was roaring into the driveway on the farm motorbike, barely putting the stand down before he came running into the kitchen.

"You all right, love?" he called out for Joan, who was now sweeping up the ash from around the fireplace.

"Oh my God, David, did you feel THAT?" She held out her arms and David pulled her into a warm embracing hug.

"Christ, it was pretty big, ae? I was worried the walls might come down round ya."

"Nah, just the chimney!" Joan smiled up at him. "The little house held on tight and kept me safe." She buried her face into his chest, and for a moment I wondered what might have become of me, and Joan, had my walls fallen down. I thought about Jim and felt grateful he had built me with such care and attention. I was just a shoe box compared to some of the houses on this road, and yet, once again, I had kept my inhabitants safe from harm.

It felt bittersweet knowing that in just a few weeks Joan and David would leave me for their new home up the road, in time for when the baby came.

David became increasingly worried about their finances and being able to provide for the impending arrival, and one night when they were discussing what was needed, David brought up the idea of selling Joan's surfboard.

"No way, David, I am not selling it!" Joan shook her head adamantly.

"What's wrong with you, Joanie? We need a bloody baby bassinet! What're you gonna keep it in, a bloody shoe box?" Joan fixed her stare into the corner of the room and crossed her arms.

Back and forth the argument went, with David trying to reason with Joan, their voices becoming more and more raised.

"No! I don't want to sell it, all right? It's my bab…" Joan suddenly stopped short as she realised her surfboard, her 'baby', was, in only a matter of weeks, going to be replaced by a very real baby. Her eyes filled with tears as she knew her husband was right.

David's face softened as he looked at his young wife, and he reached an arm across to touch her tenderly on the shoulder.

"Look, we'll just sell it now while we need the money for the bassinet, and when we've moved into the big house and saved some more money, we can buy another one, all right?"

"Fine." Joan shrugged his hand off her shoulder and got up and left the room.

In the bedroom, Joan lay down on their bed and cried into her pillow. I sensed it was more than just the surfboard, though. Life was changing. And in a big way for all of us. It was scary and tense, and I was worried about them leaving me. Who would come and live here next?

As Joan fell asleep on her side, I watched her chest rise and fall and felt comforted by the sight, my own eaves rising and falling with her every breath.

A few weeks later, after the selling of the surfboard and the purchase of the new bassinet, things seemed back on track, and Joan and David began to excitedly pack up their things to move to their new home up the road.

While they were in the process of packing, Jack bought another couple around to look me over.

The man, Carl, was big and burly, with a tight black singlet pulled over his belly, and long hair to his shoulders. His partner, Amy, was small and blonde, and rather subdued, walking around the rooms at a slight pace behind them.

"I like what you've done with the place," Amy said shyly, stopping to watch Joan fold up the linen.

"Thanks!" Joan shot her a big smile. "We've loved living here, she's a fine little house. I'm sure you'll be very happy!"

"Yes… I…" Amy looked at Joan and then cast her eyes quickly out of the room towards the bedroom where her partner was. "I hope so, we've… we've just moved around so much."

Joan's brow furrowed at this comment, and she watched Amy leave the room quietly, almost mouse-like, following behind her boyfriend as he walked outside into the garden.

When they had left, Joan expressed concern to David.

"Something's not right with those two. I could sense it straight away."

"Yeah, I felt it too," David replied. "But ya know, don't judge a book by its cover and all that."

He smiled at Joan and pulled her close. "It's our last night in this little house. Let's make the most of it, shall we? I got us one of those pies you like from the store; we could put some music on and light the candles…"

He gave her a knowing smile and Joan giggled like a schoolgirl, reaching up on tiptoes to kiss him, getting in as close as her belly would allow. Their last night within my walls was filled with love and laughter, memories I would grow to cherish.

How different this was to what was about to come.

Chapter 5

At first, things seemed pretty normal. Carl and Amy moved in, unpacked what meagre things they had, and settled in. It was only after about the first week that I realised something was not right between them.

Carl had just come in from the pub and Amy was dishing up his dinner.

"It's cold," was the first thing he said to her as he spooned some of the mashed potato into his mouth.

"Sorry, love, but you said you'd be home at six-thirty. It's seven now."

"So?" Carl screwed his face up at her. "What the fuck difference does that make? The dinner shoulda stayed in the oven, then."

Amy bit her lip and looked down at her plate. "Yes... but last time I did that, you said the dinner was too dry. So I..."

"So I...," Carl imitated her. "So you decided to give it to me cold instead."

"I'm sorry!" Amy's voice was barely a whisper. "I can put it back in the oven then if you want it hotter?"

Carl picked up the plate, held his arm out, and in one movement tipped the plate and its contents upside down onto the carpet.

I was flabbergasted! I had never seen someone react in such a way.

"I don't want it dry or cold! I just wanna proper decent meal for once in ma fucking life!"

With that, he pushed back his chair and got up from the table. He walked around the table to where Amy sat, shaking now in her chair, and leaned right down over her so that his face was next to hers.

"Tomorrow night, you will cook me a decent dinner, and whether I am early, late or whatever the fuck, you will have it ready for me or else. You got it?"

Amy nodded her head.

Carl slammed the flat of his hand down onto the table in an almighty thump that made both Amy and I jump. "I said, you got it?"

"Yes, yes, of course. I'm sorry!" Amy kept her head down, staring at her plate.

"I'm going out for fish and chips. You can eat ya fucking shit food." And with that, Carl stomped out the door, revved the engine of his Cortina and exited the drive in a spray of gravel.

Amy sat there, her head still bowed, breathing hard for a minute or two. When she looked up, I could see her eyes were slightly moist with tears, yet she brushed back her hair, took a deep breath in, and continued eating her food as if nothing had happened.

After dinner, Amy cleaned up the mess, did the dishes, lit a cigarette, and curled up in the corner chair to read a magazine, occasionally looking up at the door, as if waiting for Carl to return at any minute.

In the end, after hours of waiting, she got up, brushed her teeth and washed her face and crawled into their cold, empty bed.

Carl returned home in the early hours of the morning, stumbling into the bedroom and falling under the covers, snoring loudly, with his arm draped lazily over Amy's small frame.

I noticed her eyes were open and blinking in the darkness like two small beads. Amy continued staring ahead at the wall, awake until the first grey light of dawn.

In the morning, Amy got up and cooked the two of them breakfast. Eggs and bacon, toast and tomatoes, the zip on the boil to make tea. Carl came wandering into the kitchen rubbing his bloodshot eyes, his clothes crumpled from sleeping in them.

"Morning, love." He gave Amy a kiss on the head, who stopped in her tracks to allow this gesture.

"Morning," she replied, pouring his tea and setting it down next to the steaming plate of food.

They ate virtually in silence, Carl looking at the sports section of the *Daily News*, Amy looking out at the garden.

Once they were finished, Carl rose from his seat, wiped his mouth and took his dishes to the sink.

"Righto then, I better get going. See ya later on."

"OK, bye."

As soon as the car had left the driveway, Amy exhaled, and reached for her cigarettes.

She spent the day tidying round the house, washing clothes and hanging them out to dry in the cool autumn breeze. Sometimes she would just stop what she was doing and stare into the distance, as if trying to remember where she was.

That night, Amy prepared the dinner slowly. Taking her time, and leaving everything to the last minute, so that whatever time Carl returned, she could have the dinner into the oven as quickly as possible.

However, this made no difference. Carl was late home again, and as soon as he came into the kitchen I could tell he had been drinking.

"Ah… have you been at the pub?" Amy asked.

"Yeah, so what? Where's dinner?"

"It's nearly done." Amy gestured towards the oven. "So, you making some new friends then?"

"What's it to ya?" Carl frowned. "Better fucking company than YOU, that's for sure!"

"I was only asking; you don't have to say that to me." Amy turned her back on him as she pulled the plates out of the cupboard.

Carl rose to his feet again.

"What the fuck did you just say to me?"

"Nothing, babe, it's nothing. Sit back down and I'll bring you a beer." Amy kept her back to him, but I could see her face etched in a mixture of anger and fear.

"I'll sit back down if I fucking want!" Carl walked over to where Amy stood in front of the cupboard, her head down, busying herself with the plates.

I watched his hand come up from his side swiftly, and he suddenly slammed Amy's head into the cupboard door. Amy gasped, and I rattled my roof in anger. What on earth was that for?

Carl sneered as Amy teetered back on her feet, reaching out to clutch the kitchen bench to stop herself from falling.

"Don't fucking tell me what to do, bitch, all right? Just get me my dinner and shut the fuck up."

He turned away from her, pulling a beer out of the fridge as he walked past, before setting himself down in front of their black and white television.

Amy steadied herself, her hand on her forehead where she had connected with the cupboard. A huge red lump was rising fast. But she shook her head, and carried on, pulling the food out of the oven and getting it onto the dining table for him as quickly as possible.

I had never seethed so much in my life. Watching them eat, Amy was obviously in pain, but Carl continued on oblivious, or if not oblivious, then not caring, ranting on about some guy at the pub who was giving him grief at work.

Towards the end of their meal, Amy rose to her feet. "I'm sorry, I need to lie down. I feel dizzy."

As she tried to stand, Carl grabbed her by her arm and pulled her onto his lap.

"Come on now and give me a kiss goodnight before you go anywhere." He grabbed her face in his hands and tried to kiss her. Amy pulled away.

"Please, don't, I feel like I might be sick." As she strained to avoid his lips, Carl pushed her off his lap and onto the floor.

"What, I make you sick, is that it?"

"No, Carl! The fucking bump on my head that you gave me makes me feel sick!" Amy shouted at him from the floor. I had never heard her raise her voice at him, and I instantly felt very afraid for her.

"Don't you fucking even…" Carl's foot kicked out at her from where he sat and caught her clean on the jaw. Amy fell back onto the carpet, and as she struggled to sit up, Carl came at her again, this time with an open hand. He slapped her hard across the face, one of his nails catching her lip, which sprouted blood. Amy cried out, but this didn't deter him; he put his foot into the side of her ribs and sent her sprawling onto her stomach.

While she lay there crying and shaking, Carl just looked at her with absolute disgust. If only he knew how I looked at him the same way. He turned on his heels and walked out the front door and was back in the car and gone again.

Alone with Amy, I longed to be able to console her, to ease her pain and fear. But all I could do was pull my walls in close, to try and make her feel safe, but I knew it was to no avail.

This was not something I could protect her from, and almost every night Amy endured his beatings, as I endured watching them.

Week after week, Carl would come home drunk. It was a wonder he could get the car up the road and into the driveway. And always he would find something wrong with things Amy said or did that would set him off in a rage of punches, slaps, kicks or verbal abuse.

No wonder Amy never left the house. Her face was often covered in bruises or welts.

One afternoon when Carl was at work and Amy was outside hanging up her washing, to my delight Joan called in. And she had brought her little baby son with her.

I flapped my doors and windows in delight, relishing in the wind that aided my show of happiness. Amy stood rigid with fear, poised behind the washing line, listening as she heard the crunch of tyres on the driveway.

"Oh! You scared me!" Amy broke into a smile as Joan peeked her head around the washing line.

"Hello! Sorry! I didn't mean to frighten you. I just thought I would call in and say hello and see how you were getting on in the little house! Got everything you need?"

Amy was so visibly relieved and ecstatic to see someone other than Carl appear, she practically dragged Joan and her baby into the house for a cup of tea.

"He's so gorgeous!" Amy eyed up the baby enviously. "What's his name?"

Joan jiggled him round on her lap. "His name is Harley, aren't you, darling? He's such a good baby. Sleeps loads and is full of smiles!" She looked up from her son and her own smile dropped as she noticed for the first time the blue bruise that spread across Amy's jaw. "Oh! What happened to your poor face?"

Amy's fingers flew to the bruise. She felt its pain under the tips of her fingers. "It's nothing. I just caught my face on the side of the bookshelf."

"The bookshelf? Ouch, it looks so painful! You should put some ice on that, it will ease the swelling." Joan and Amy's eyes locked for a minute in a gaze that said a thousand words.

I can see he has punched you. I know you are scared. You should leave him.

But Joan said nothing. She looked back down at her baby boy, and thanked her lucky stars David was a good man to her. He may have sworn at her in anger now and then, but he had never so much as raised a finger to her.

"Here's the tea," Amy smiled brightly and set down two cups for them to enjoy.

In the next half an hour they talked about Joan's new house and garden, how big it was and all their plans for more children. I didn't feel envious of Joan and David's new home; I was happy for them. But I was envious of the life that was lived between their new home's walls. I missed that happiness. All I felt with Amy and Carl was sadness and lots and lots of anger and fear.

Just before Joan left, she wrote a number on a piece of paper and handed it to Amy.

"This is my doctor in Kaponga. He is a very nice man and if you ever need him for anything, or to look at anything..." Her eyes darted towards Amy's bruise. "Well, he makes house calls, and would be more than happy to help you, I'm sure."

She pulled the now sleeping Harley up into her arms. 'And I am only down the road if you ever want to visit, or need anything from us." She gave Amy a quick peck on the cheek and walked off down the road. Amy waved at her until she was just a speck in the distance, turning the piece of paper with the doctor's number on it over and over in her hands.

Chapter 6

Over the following weeks, there were some days when you would think nothing seemed the matter. Carl and Amy would wake in the morning, have their breakfast, and go about their business as usual.

But always when Carl drank he turned into a monster and Amy would be at the mercy of his fury. I wished so much that Amy would just leave. But they only had one car, and apart from Joan, who had not been back to visit, Amy had no friends either.

One particularly vicious beating left Amy with a gaping sore in the side of her arm where he had taken to her with his belt buckle. The wound obviously needed stitches, but Carl refused to take her to the doctor. Instead, he told her to 'harden up', and went off out to Opunake to watch the rugby. Her arm continued to throb and seep through the ridiculously small plaster she had applied, and, feeling desperate, Amy reached for the number of the doctor that Joan had recommended, and called him.

It turned out that the doctor was about to make a house call to a family who lived not far from Amy, and he would be able to call in and see her as soon as he had made his first visit.

Within the hour, Doctor Corby was at the door. Handsome and well dressed, and in his early forties, Doctor Corby gently stitched Amy's arm and applied a bandage, before giving her a tetanus shot, as Amy had 'cut it on a corrugated fence'.

"So, is everything else all right here, Miss Irving?" Doctor Corby smiled gently as Amy shyly looked away.

"Yes... everything is fine, thank you."

No, it's not all right! I wanted to shout. Tell him what has been happening!

But the doctor left, and Amy was alone again. Her tiny frame seemed even smaller. Her pretty features tired and worn, she collapsed in her chair and lit a cigarette.

"One day I will leave him," she suddenly said out loud. "I will either kill the bastard or I will walk outta here."

Do it! I wanted to say. I expanded and retracted my walls in a breath of frustration.

"Woah, what the fuck?" Amy leapt up, her cigarette still burning between her fingers. "Who's there?" She scanned the room, her eyes darting back and forth. "Hello? Doctor?"

I was silent. I forgot that sometimes my noises could be alarming. The last thing I wanted to do was scare her as well!

Amy sat back down gingerly, her eyes still flickering distrustfully. Eventually, when she had finished her cigarette and relaxed a little, she closed her eyes and allowed herself to doze.

Suddenly, the car was in the driveway and Amy sat up, alert. She glanced at the clock on the wall and immediately I sensed danger. It was six o'clock and dinner wasn't on, Carl was back from the rugby, and no doubt drunk.

With that, the front door swung open and Carl stood looming in the doorway, his huge shoulders blocking out the late winter sun that was just shrinking behind the hedge.

"Where are ya?" was the first thing he said as he stumbled into the room. Even through my walls, I could smell the alcohol that radiated off him.

"Carl, I'm just about to get the dinner on!" Amy was up and out of her seat and into the kitchen, where she began pulling food out of the freezer at lightning pace.

"What the hell, Amy? I'm hungry now! It's six o'clock, dinner should be ON!"

"Carl, I know, I'm sorry, but the painkillers the doctor gave me made me a bit sleepy and I..."

"You've been asleep. Fucking typical. Trust you, on the one night that I am home when you insist I be, and you don't even have dinner ready for me... Wait... what doctor?" Carl spun around, his eyes narrowing. "You went to see the doctor?"

"No, the... um... the doctor came here. I needed him to see to my... my arm..." She trailed off, realising the more she said, the worse it would make things.

I hoped that he was so drunk that he might just topple over and pass out where he fell, but no such luck. He began to rant and shout at Amy, standing there telling her no fucking doctor should have been called without him, and how much was it going to bloody cost?

The front door was still wide open, the cold air seeping in, his bellowing voice echoing out into the paddocks.

Amy continued to rush around, turning on the oven, pulling frozen mince out of its bag and into a pan, all the while wincing in pain from her bandaged arm.

"Ya devious bitch! Calling the doctor once I'm gone! You know what, though, ya fucking useless, Amy, you're a stupid, dumb, thick-as-shit piece of arse that no one in their right mind would wanna marry! I don't even know what I'm doing with you, you fucking whore! Inviting doctors in here so you can what, ae? Try and get a bit a sympathy? You fucking…"

Right at that moment, Amy swung round with the pan in her hand and struck Carl hard across the head. He stopped talking immediately and just stood there, dazed, in absolute shock.

I don't think Amy could quite believe it herself either. She looked aghast at the pan in her hand, as if it were completely foreign to her. The consequences of her actions suddenly becoming very apparent as the blood rose in Carl's already swollen face.

"YOU FUCKING BITCH! I'M GONNA KILL YOU!" Carl roared, and lunged for Amy, his face a contorted ball of steaming anger. Amy screamed in horror and leapt out of his way, avoiding his drunken grasp. She ran into the bedroom to get away, but before she could shut the door behind her she tripped and went flying across the floor. Carl staggered towards the bedroom, one of his clenched fists pounding the palm of the other. "You are SO gonna get it this time!"

Amy scrambled desperately across the floor towards the door, and, as Carl neared, I felt myself rise up from my foundations in anger and I rattled my hinges with all of my might.

The bedroom door slammed shut in his face and I tried to hold it fast for as long as I could. On the other side of the door, Carl looked dumbfounded at the self-slamming door and began to kick and pound on it, tugging at the handle that I kept stuck fast.

"Help me!" screamed Amy. "Someone help me!" She threw open the window in the bedroom and continued to scream, as Carl threw his weight against the door. Though I tried to hold fast, my tiny plywood door was no match for his weight. In he tumbled, and he was straight on his feet, grabbing Amy by the hair and pulling her out into the lounge, where she screamed and kicked, trying to free herself from his grasp.

"You tried to kill me, you bitch!" He raised his fist and smashed it hard into her face, her nose bleeding instantly. Pulling Amy by the hair again, he bashed her head into the side of the coffee table several times, almost knocking her out in the process, before stopping to rant and spit anger at her with a venom I had never known between my walls before.

"Stop what you're doing right now!" a man's voice shouted from the front door.

Turning on his heel, Carl came face to face with the barrel of a shotgun hoisted on the shoulder of none other than his landlord, Jack Barry. Behind him, outside on the step, was Ruth, and out in the driveway stood Doctor Corby.

"It's got nuthin' to do with you, Jack, mate," Carl growled slowly, instinctively raising his arms to the ceiling. "Just a little argument between me and my girl is all."

"Looks a lot more than that to me... *mate*," Jack replied with gritted teeth, his shotgun unwavering. "Now back away from Amy and let her come to me. Amy, come here to me, love!" Jack's gaze dropped down to where a barely-conscious Amy struggled to stand; but, as he took his eyes off Carl, in an instant Carl had grabbed a knife from the counter and had it at Amy's throat.

"You fucking touch her and I'll kill her!"

Jack brought the gun back up, but backed away slightly, unsure of what to do now.

"Calm down, mate, it's all good. I'm not gonna shoot you. Just let her go, yeah? Come on, mate, you're drunk, it's all a misunderstanding," Jack reasoned.

"You bet it's a fucking misunderstanding!" Carl yelled. "Get the fuck out of my house or I will cut this bitch's throat!"

"Jack!" came Ruth's anxious voice from out on the step.

"Stay outside, love, it's all under control," Jack shouted over his shoulder.

Amy whimpered slightly in Carl's grip. Her legs were jelly, but she had no strength to stand. Carl was trying to hold her up, and keep the knife to her throat at the same time.

I watched as, outside, Doctor Corby came around the back, surveying my windows, before spotting the small opened window in the bedroom.

While the two men squared off in the lounge and Jack continued to try to reason with Carl, Doctor Corby shimmied in through the bedroom window, grabbed the heaviest object he could find (which was the iron) and tiptoed through the bedroom door into the lounge.

"Hey, Carl!"

Surprised, Carl turned towards the sound of the doctor's voice and, as he did so, Doctor Corby swung the iron across the side of his head, knocking him out, and onto the floor.

Jack and Ruth rushed forward and Amy fell into Ruth's arms, crying hysterically.

"Shh now, love, it's all right, it's all over... it's all over."

Jack gave the doctor a grim smile. "Nice one, mate."

Doctor Corby smiled back and shrugged his shoulders. "No worries. I think that's what they mean when they say 'just what the doctor ordered'." The two men smirked, but were both visibly shaken. The police were called, and they escorted a still-unconscious Carl away in an ambulance.

It turned out Doctor Corby had been having a cup of tea with Jack and Ruth when they heard the commotion and came rushing down to Amy's rescue. The doctor saw to Amy's cuts and bruises, before they took her into Hawera to a women's shelter for the night.

When everyone was gone and I was on my own again, I felt a huge wave of relief wash over me. As if in empathy, it began to rain outside. A light pattering on my roof that felt like the tears I could not otherwise express. I had never known such violence and sadness, and hoped that I would never have to bear witness to such events again. Whoever lived within my walls next could surely not be as bad? I lay in hope.

Chapter 7

It was over a year before Jack found anyone to rent me. A few people came through, but no one ever seemed to like me. I was either 'too small' or 'too near the road' or 'in the middle of nowhere'. I felt tainted. After she came with a friend one day to quickly collect her things, I never saw Amy again, but I hoped that she was now free of Carl's clutches and living a happier life. As for him, I was sure he would be punished for all those years of abuse.

At least, I hoped so.

While I was on my own, I took the time to search what memory I had of 'before', to see if I could remember my existence pre-cottage. The images and feelings I had were becoming stronger now, and I repeated them over and over, as if etching them into my wood with a hot poker.

I could remember the sound of the wind as it weaved its way through what I felt surely now must have been my branches, and I recalled the sight of the leaves that rustled and fell like glitter from my canopy to the forest floor below. Mount Taranaki, always strong and steadfast as my view both before and now, continued to be a beacon of belonging to me. However, from where I sat now, I could see that shimmering haze of blue in the distance towards the West that lay parallel to the sky. And still I puzzled over what it was.

Sometimes, especially over the winter, I just retreated into a kind of peaceful darkness. After the intensity of Carl and Amy's relationship within my walls, I was grateful for the serenity.

But I did miss people's conversations, and the sound of laughter. The warmth of the fire when it was roaring, and the smell of dinner in the oven.

One early morning, as a late winter frost was giving over to the tentative rays of the sunrise, a car with a large trailer backed up and into my driveway.

A couple and their two young children got out, blinking in the early-morning light. Their breath hung in the frosty air and they looked tired and crumpled, as if they had been driving all night.

"Is this it, Daddy?" the little boy whispered. "Is this the new house?"

"Yes, son, this is it." The father spoke with a lilt to his voice, evidence of his foreign background. He had a long, bushy, black beard and thick black hair. His wife was also dark-haired, and long and lean. She, however, spoke with a New Zealand accent. This, I soon learned, was Fernand and Marleen Halden and their two children, Francia and Mark.

They had come from a place called Levin, a few hours south of Taranaki, and had indeed set out early in darkness. Their arrival was quiet and slow-paced, the family taking their time to unload things, and determine where in the house they would go.

74

"It's much smaller than I imagined it to be," Marleen said, as she walked from room to room. "And quite haphazard in its arrangement."

"Yes, it's definitely had its share of bits added on," Fernand echoed her thoughts, as he followed after her, placing boxes here and there.

Fernand reached his arm out and pulled his wife in for a quick hug.

"I know it's not much, but it will have to do until I'm earning enough that we can find a house we can afford in town."

Marleen stiffened at his touch and for a moment I feared that this was in the same way Amy would freeze whenever Carl had tried to hug her. However, as she pulled away from him, Marleen looked calm and unfazed. It was Fernand, meanwhile, who looked back at her with a wounded look.

Ruth and Jack arrived after breakfast to welcome the couple to their new home.

I always delighted in seeing them, though I noticed that both were starting to look rather tired and aged.

They sat and had a cup of tea with their new tenants while the children moved politely about their bedrooms, unpacking books and toys.

"So, you start the job on Monday then, is it?" Jack enquired. "You'll be pleased to get into it, I imagine, and so will all the farmers up that road. It's been nothing but a bumpy old gravel track for years."

"Yes, I am looking forward to it, thank you," Fernand replied, thoughtfully stroking his beard. "It will be a change working on the roads up here, especially with that as the view." He gestured out the window towards the mountain.

"And your little ones will be going to Awatuna Primary." Ruth beamed at Marleen. "It's a lovely school, and the new library being built is going to make it even better."

Marleen gave a tight smile, and looked slightly bored. "Yes, I suppose… So, is there anything to actually DO in this place?" She said the words 'this place' as if she had only at the last minute decided to miss out the words 'God forsaken'.

Ruth knitted her brows together as she quickly thought of things that might interest Marleen.

"Well, there is Women's Division, and the Floral Art Club. We sometimes have things through the church, and they are always in need of people to help with relief reading at the school."

"Plus Kaponga is only ten minutes' drive away and, of course, Opunake to the West," Jack chimed in. "The Club Hotel is a nice pub in town, good for a beer, if you want to come." He nodded at Fernand, but before he had a chance to reply, Marleen cut in.

"Oh, he won't want to go to the pub, will you, Fernand? He barely drinks, or smokes, or does anything that might be considered fun or naughty." She rolled her eyes and sat back in her chair, staring at her husband, who shifted uncomfortably in his seat.

I watched as for a few seconds the couples sat there without a word. I saw Ruth and Jack exchange an awkward glance, before Jack broke the silence.

"Ah, come now, you don't need to drink to enjoy it. There's a pool table! And darts too."

He grinned at Fernand encouragingly, who returned Jack's smile.

"Well, thank you, Jack; perhaps I may take you up on that offer one day."

With that, he stood and set about clearing the cups and saucers, as Jack motioned at Ruth they should probably get going.

When Jack and Ruth had begun walking up the road back towards the big house, Fernand turned to his wife and glared.

"I would prefer it if you didn't put me down like that in front of our guests, Marleen. You make me sound like a bore!"

Marleen huffed at him. "Well, it's true, isn't it? You promised me after everything that we would do more things together, have more fun and excitement. And instead you just moved us to the middle of nowhere."

Fernand moved across the room and stood eye to eye with his wife.

"Everything I have ever done I have done for you and our children. I tried to give us the best I could in Levin, and you know it. I never did anything I shouldn't... It was you that had the... the..." His jaw worked back and forth as he struggled to find the words.

Marleen waited, and when nothing came, she rolled her eyes again.

"Exactly. You never did *anything*. For the love of God, Fernand, grow a backbone! If you had one in the first place, then maybe it never would have happened."

Fernand's cheeks reddened as though he had been slapped.

Marleen turned on her heels and headed into her daughter's room, who was still quietly going about putting things here and there.

"Oh, look at you! You've practically unpacked the whole room on your own!"

Meanwhile, Fernand still stood there, his jaw clenching and unclenching. He waited until his breathing had slowed and turned and left the room, shutting the bedroom door silently behind him.

Spring took its hold on the landscape around me. There was always a lot of rain at this time of year, but whenever it cleared, the sun would shine bright and strong, and everything seemed to flourish tenfold. The grass in the hay paddock next to me grew long and green, the sweet smell of its crushed stalks lingering in the air, as the Halden children raced through it, laughing in the sunshine.

Marleen took a job up at the primary school doing relief reading, which seemed to keep her busy and seemed to satisfy Fernand also. He worked long hours on the roads up near the mountain's bush line, driving the roller that crushed the new road into a flat, smooth surface.

They bickered frequently, but sometimes Marleen seemed to soften, and would allow Fernand to drape an arm around her when they were sitting on the sofa watching television after dinner.

For the most part, their lives were taken up with their new jobs and looking after the children.

Marleen made a few friends with some of the mothers up at the school, including a pregnant Joan, who paid a visit to Marleen one Saturday with Harley and her infant son Luke.

I was pleased to see them and especially Luke, whom I had not seen before, and was delighted to hear how Joan and David were getting on in their home and working the farm.

"It does feel like the middle of nowhere sometimes," Joan nodded sympathetically as Marleen explained how she was finding Awatuna very different to Levin. "But you get used to it, and you make friends."

"But nothing ever seems to happen around here!" Marleen shook her head, exasperated. "Don't you get bored?" She turned the tap on a cask of wine and poured them both a small glass, which Luke, who was on Joan's knee, immediately reached for.

"Ah ah, not for you!" Joan swooped the glass out of reach and took a sip, instead putting a soft rattle into his outstretched fingers.

"Francia! Mark! Harley! Come take the bubba for a walk out to see the cows, would you? The Mummies need to talk." As Marleen called, the children obediently came out of Mark's bedroom, where they had been playing.

"Don't go near the road, okay? Just stay out the back, there's a good boy." Joan popped a kiss on Harley's forehead and handed Luke over to Francia, who tenderly hoisted him onto her hip.

"God, my two are just as exciting as their father." Marleen lowered her voice as the children headed outside. "I wouldn't mind if they acted up occasionally or gave me cause for concern; but no, they just read and do homework and act like robots." She shook her head and raised her glass to her lips.

"Some mothers would kill for kids that well behaved!" laughed Joan. "So, how are you finding working at the school?" Joan asked, changing the subject. "That must keep you busy, no?"

Marleen smiled slyly and tipped her head to the side.

"I tell you what, working alongside that Principal Grey certainly makes it a lot easier." She flicked her eyebrows knowingly and took another gulp of wine.

Joan laughed nervously. "What do you mean?" Although she knew perfectly well what Marleen meant.

"Well, he's easy on the eye and he's very... shall we say... accommodating to whatever I might need." She laughed a throaty laugh, tossing her head back so you could see her silver fillings.

Joan smiled a tight smile and didn't say anything. I could tell she didn't like Marleen very much.

I wasn't sure I liked Marleen much either. However, I also knew from many conversations between the Haldens, and between Marleen and Joan, that Marleen's resentment of her husband and her life wasn't entirely without reason.

Marleen had met Fernand when she was nineteen and travelling through Germany. She had left school the previous year and used inheritance money from her grandparents to buy a ticket to see the world – before (as she had promised her parents) she returned and attended university.

Marleen described herself as a 'carefree young woman of the sixties', travelling through country after country with her bag on her back, falling in love with Artists and Musicians she met along the way, dancing under stars, and sleeping on beaches with those whom she made friends.

I listened as she told Joan the story of how she had met Fernand one night in a bar in Hamburg. A country boy who had come to town for a night out with friends.

"Of course, he was absolutely gorgeous, but as innocent as a child. I felt he needed breaking in!" She laughed at her description of him, and how she had gone back with him to her tiny apartment and slept with him. "It was terrible, like sleeping with a very nervous plank!"

However, despite this, he stayed at her apartment the next three days, where they continued to make love, eat breakfast together in bed, and talk about their respective lives. When her days in Hamburg were up, they said their goodbyes without exchanging addresses (Marleen didn't see the point), and she continued on her travels.

Joan leaned in now, listening intently as Marleen then explained how she had discovered she was pregnant when she was at a retreat halfway up a mountain in Bulgaria, and cried non-stop, realising she had no idea how she was supposed to have a termination while travelling.

"I guess I just ignored it, hoping it would go away. I should have gone home, but then my parents would want to know why I was cutting my trip short. I thought perhaps if I went back to Germany, Fernand might help me, he might know someone; but it took me weeks to locate him, as he was constantly away working. By the time I got in touch with him and he took me to a doctor, they said I was past the date of termination and I would have to keep the baby.

"That's when Fernand offered to support me. He said he would marry me and even move back to New Zealand if I wanted. It was a hugely generous offer; I could see he was so into me. I think it made me resent him even more. His kindness, and readiness to be with me."

Joan's face softened as she obviously thought of Marleen and Fernand weighing up their options a world away in Germany. Perhaps she was thinking how they were all just children really, similar to when she fell pregnant from David.

But, I thought, at least Joan and David had been in love, and David had already proposed before she got pregnant.

"So we came back to New Zealand. I told my parents I had fallen in love with Fernand and we were going to have a baby and get married, and while they were surprised and a bit disappointed, they still supported me, and appreciated Fernand for supporting me too. Dad helped Fernand get a job working for the Ministry of Transport, grading and rolling the roads; and me, well, that was my university plans crushed."

I knew Joan would sympathise with this part of the story especially. She too had harboured plans to go to Teachers' College, but that was on hold now that she was wife and mother. And being a farmer's wife meant she had to be a mum, look after the house and be on the farm at times too.

"I sometimes have a little time to work on my paintings, but not as much as I used to," Joan admitted. "David needs me to help with feeding the calves, and, of course, soon there'll be two little boys running round, not to mention a new one too!" She patted her stomach affectionately.

I watched these two women talking and thought about my own 'Life'. I had certainly not found it boring since I had been moved here. My walls had seen and heard things that would stay with me forever, and if I could talk, a thousand secrets, wishes and fears would come tumbling out.

My life, and my stories, mostly consisted of those that inhabited me, and I wondered if other houses had the same experiences, or could feel and think in the same way I could.

Joan came to visit now and then, but I sensed that Marleen often rubbed her the wrong way. Joan had always been a sensitive soul, and while she and David obviously had their ups and downs, there had been no mistaking their love for one another.

Marleen was so obvious in her 'tolerance' of Fernand, who, while a good husband and father, definitely did not provide Marleen with the exciting life she had once had for herself, and her straight-up comments regarding this often made Joan and some of her other friends uncomfortable. Still, such was the isolation these women found themselves in at times, even those they did not like so much were still needed to help fill out their friendship group, and Marleen was one of those.

One afternoon, when Marleen was home from school and getting the evening's dinner ready, and the two children were sitting at the dining room table finishing their homework, Fernand came home from work a couple of hours early. As he walked in the door, I could tell something was the matter. On the radio the soft strains of 'The First Time Ever I Saw Your Face' by Roberta Flack were gently filling the room, but this was quickly drowned out by Fernand's solid and meaningful steps into the house.

"Oh! You're home early," Marleen exclaimed, looking up from the potatoes she was peeling.

"Marleen, I need to have a word with you right now in the bedroom, if you don't mind."

The children looked up from their homework, but their father barely glanced at them.

"*Now, please!*" His voice was strained, on the point of breaking, as if he may shout or cry.

Marleen put the potato peeler onto the bench and wiped her hands on the tea towel.

"Finish up your work, kids, and then you can put the telly on." She gave them a tight-lipped smile and followed her husband into the bedroom, closing the door softly behind them.

"What's the matter?" she asked, confused and suddenly nervous. "Has something happened?"

"What has *happened*…" Fernand turned to face her, his brows now bent in anger. "Is that I have just found out that you have been carrying on behind my back with the bloody principal of the school our bloody children go to!" His hands were gesticulating wildly in front of his face, his fingertips full of the rage he was trying to contain. "Why are you doing this to me? To us! I thought we left this kind of, of, *behaviour* behind us when we left Levin! But no, even though I bring you to the middle of the bloody countryside, you still…" He dropped his head into his hands and rubbed his face, as if trying to blot out some terrible image he had in his mind.

"What are you talking about?" Marleen shook her head in confusion and anger. "I am NOT carrying on with any bloody one! Principal Grey is just a nice guy whom I happen to get on with and who makes my day that bit better doing that tedious bloody job! That is all!"

"Marleen, Robert Johnston *saw you*. He was dropping his kids to school and he said he saw you and the Principal…"

"Who the fuck is Robert Johnston?" Marleen cut in, Fernand flinching as she cursed in this way. "Who in the hell is *he* to say this about me?"

"I work with him, Marleen. He saw you both cuddling, and he said he had heard whispers as well, and he felt he had to tell me because…"

"Because people have nothing better to do in this shit-hole place than gossip and tell bullshit LIES!"

Marleen's voice was raised now, her eyes on fire as she stared at her husband.

"You can think what you want, Fernand, but it's not true. I promised you before that I wouldn't do anything ever again, and I have kept that promise." She narrowed her eyes and in a voice as thick with hate as she could muster, added, "As bloody boring and depressing as it has been having to."

At that last comment, Fernand's jaw dropped. In that moment, watching them argue, I understood that it suddenly occurred to him that it didn't actually matter whether or not Marleen was having another affair. The fact was, she considered her life with him to be boring and depressing and there was nothing he could ever do to change her opinion of him or that fact.

He held her gaze steadily and calmly. "Then why are you even still here, Marleen? Why are either of us?"

"Because… the children, of course." She gave a half-hearted shrug.

"And what else, Marleen? If your life with me is so hopeless, then why don't you just take the kids and go back to Levin?" He waited and looked at her, imploring her to say the words that would convince him she loved him and needed him and wanted to be with him. But Marleen said nothing.

Fernand just shook his head, picked up his jacket and, giving each of his children a kiss on the head, left the house and got into their car, leaving without another word.

Marleen sat on the bed and began to cry. Soft muffled sobs at first and then huge gasping ones, where I feared she might suffocate herself. Francia and Mark came and stood silently at the door, watching their mother as she cried into her pillow and beat it with her fists.

"I didn't bloody do anything!" she yelled into the bedclothes. "Why can't people just mind their own bloody business?"

That night, Fernand never came home. Once Marleen had gathered herself together and poured a glass of wine and got the children their dinner, she sat in the corner of the lounge with the light off, waiting for Fernand to return. Though she sat in darkness, I could see her face. At first it was crumpled in anger, but then, as the night wore on and still he did not return, it became etched in worry. Eventually, at some point, Marleen fell asleep, and when she awoke, confused as to where she was, her neck stiff with the morning chill, she pulled herself out of her chair and went into their bedroom. The bed lay as before, the sheets and cover crinkled from where she had beat them with her fists, her pillowcase stained with mascara from her tears.

"Perhaps he fell asleep in his car somewhere," she murmured aloud, but I did not think she was convinced by this.

That morning, Marleen got the children up for school, telling them their father had stayed at a friend's, and then phoned the school to tell them she wouldn't be coming in. I could hear in her voice the humiliation she felt that perhaps people were indeed talking about her, but I also could see how tired she was from the events the night before.

After the children had gone off to school on the bus, Marleen lay back down on the bed and closed her eyes. However, both she and I jumped at the sound of the phone ringing in the front room.

"Hello?" Marleen was breathless as she grabbed the receiver. "Marleen Halden speaking...

"What do you mean, never showed up for work? No, he's not here. Well... I mean... I don't know where he could be... He left last night and didn't say where he was going..." Marleen's face grew more and more anxious as the call continued. "A walk in the bush? What do you mean, a walk in the bush? Who did he say that to? What bush?"

Marleen only said a few more words before she hung up the phone, picked the receiver back up and this time dialled 111.

"Hello. Police, please. I'd like to report a missing person."

Chapter 8

Police came shortly after 1pm: Constable Peter Quinn from Opunake, accompanied by another younger officer – Bradley Graham. I recognised the older man as one of the policemen who had come to take Carl away after Doctor Corby had knocked him out with the iron.

They sat on the sofa in the living room, taking notes. They had already been up to where Fernand worked to speak to his boss, as it was the last place he had been seen.

It transpired that, after arguing with Marleen, Fernand had gone back to work to finish his grading of the road. He had been pretty angry, and though his boss had said he could take the last couple of hours off, Fernand had insisted on finishing it, before saying he was going to take a walk in the bush to cool down before he headed home.

"Now, as he didn't come home last night, and didn't return to work today, we have to speculate that he has either gone walking as he intended to, and perhaps hurt himself, or got lost, or..' perhaps he has decided that he doesn't want to come home." Officer Quinn looked hard at Marleen as he said that. "Would he have any reason not to want to come home?"

Marleen hesitated and I knew she was thinking of their argument the night before, and how cruel she had been in her moment of anger.

"He thought I was… ah… he mistakenly thought that perhaps I was taking an interest in someone else." The words fell from her mouth and once they started, they didn't stop. "But he was wrong! I mean, he was right the first time, but this time he was wrong. I swear! And we argued and shouted and I told him I thought life with him was depressing and boring, but I didn't mean it! I mean, I do mean it, but it doesn't mean…" She stopped herself and looked up at the officer, her eyes brimming with tears. "Are we going to look for him?"

"Well, anyone that goes into the bushline up there by the mountain is officially stepping into the National Park. Mountain rescue has been alerted and they will take the first steps in sending out a search party on foot. We will also alert friends and family and try to see if anyone has seen or heard anything else."

The policemen got to their feet.

"If you hear or see anything leading to his whereabouts, please let us know as soon as possible," Officer Graham said, easing his hat back onto his head. "And try not to worry too much. I'm sure we'll find him."

After they had left, Marleen sat back down in the chair in the corner and stared at the spot where once a fire had taken hold of my pine wood walls.

"Is this all my fault?" she whispered aloud. "Did I make this happen?"

No, no, I wanted to say, though I felt worried for her. The sun was high and warm on my roof now. It popped and creaked in the heat. It will all be okay, I wanted to say, everything will be okay.

"I want to believe you," Marleen said aloud, before getting up and picking up the phone to call Joan. I was surprised. Had she heard me?

Joan came to sit with Marleen while they waited for news. But still there was nothing. The children came home from school and Marleen had the awful job of explaining that Daddy had gone missing. Francia began to cry and Mark just looked horrified.

"Missing, where?" he demanded. "Is this 'cause you argued?"

Suddenly, Marleen was in tears again. She looked over at Joan and then back at her son.

"Yes, it is because we argued. It's 'cause Mummy is selfish and mean and I couldn't tell Daddy how much I..." She broke off and swallowed hard. "But they are trying to find him. There are lots of people out looking for him."

This part was true. That night when Fernand did not return home again, it was in the *Daily News* the next day, spread out on the table where I could read its headline:

'Man presumed missing in Mount Egmont National Park'.

I knew just from watching the way the clouds gathered and swirled around the peak of the mountain how quickly the weather was capable of changing. One minute it would be a beautiful sunny day and then suddenly the clouds would bank up around the south of

'Fathoms Peak', the smaller of the volcanic cones, and we would be shrouded in cold cloud for the rest of the day.

I felt worried and upset for the Halden family. Marleen's parents came up from Levin and stayed with her, helping with the children as yet another day passed without word of Fernand.

"What if what the officer said is true?" I heard Marleen whisper to her mother in the garden that afternoon. "What if he isn't up the mountain, but instead… he's… he's left us?"

Marleen's mother was slightly shorter than her, but even so I could tell she once was as tall and beautiful as her daughter, her dark hair now a twist of grey and brown. She reached over and patted Marleen's hand.

"Fernand would never do that. He is a good man. If he did decide to leave, he would do it in the right way, you know that. He would see that things were left in the right way. He loves you all too much not to."

"Oh, Mum…" Marleen's face collapsed again in tears. "He is a good man, you are right. And I have just been a stupid fool! I swear nothing happened with the Principal. That morning, Rob must have just seen us hugging in hello, as we often did. We flirted a bit, and we get on really well, but nothing more. He loves his wife, and I…" She stopped and stared at the garden in silence for a moment.

Her mother and I watched her, as her private thoughts turned over in her mind.

"And I love him." She looked up at her mother, aghast at the revelation. "My God, what if he doesn't come back?"

That night, as the family slept fitfully in their beds, the police officers pulled into the driveway around 2am and knocked urgently at my front door.

Marleen leapt out of bed as if she had never been sleeping and rushed to answer the door, her nightgown flying, her face full of dread. As she opened the door and saw Constable Quinn's face, she fell against the door frame in tears. As she collapsed, I saw the policeman's face. He was smiling, and misty-eyed himself.

"They found him," he nodded. "His ankle isn't in the best shape, he's cold and tired and severely dehydrated, but they've found him."

Marleen's parents came rushing into the room in time to hear the good news, and quickly woke the children, who squealed in delight and excitement.

I banged my roof in relief and pure joy, though there was no wind or rain to hide behind. Everyone looked up at my ceiling, puzzled by the noise.

"Must be a possum up there," Officer Graham grinned.

Marleen and her father left for Taranaki Base Hospital in New Plymouth that morning to be with Fernand, leaving Marleen's mother to look after Francia and Mark.

It was another two days before their father finally came home, walking slowly up the steps using crutches and hobbling into the house. The children could barely contain their excitement, and though their mother warned them to be careful in hugging him, they threw their small arms around his waist and begged for cuddles and kisses.

Fernand looked exhausted still, his body thin and wrought from two and a half nights out in the bush. His ankle was in a splint and bandage from where he had broken it slipping into a hole. He had fallen from the path and down into a ravine.

Marleen was unlike I had ever seen her before. She fussed and fretted over Fernand, making sure he had everything he needed. She made him tea and plumped his pillows; she made his favourite dinner to help his appetite recover; and constantly asked if he was all right or wanted anything else.

That night, Fernand slept deeply, happy and relieved to be back in his bed. And though Marleen was exhausted herself from lack of sleep, she lay awake watching him, her face surveying his as though looking at him for the first time.

When Fernand woke to her smile, he reached out and touched her face, but before he could say anything she placed her finger on his lips to silence him.

"When you were lost out there, I experienced for the first time what it really felt like... the possibility that I might... lose you. Not because we had argued, or we had decided it was over, but just that circumstances could take you from me, and I might not have a choice in this.

"This scared me more than anything, because it made me realise... I do love you, Fernand.

"I have chosen to ignore this, because all I could think about was how my life could have been, how it was before, instead of focusing on what my life is now and trying to make it the best I can. By not allowing you to love me, or allowing myself to love you, I have been denying us a chance to make it better. I am so sorry for everything…" Marleen began to cry, her tears spilling down her chin. "But I swear to you, I never…"

"Shh, shh, it's OK." Fernand reached out again. "I believe you. And I'm sorry, too. I promised you I would make more of an effort to give you the kind of life you wanted, especially after everything, but instead of taking you to a place where you could thrive, I just brought you… here. Where you only struggled more. Maybe I wanted to punish you in a way, to show you I was the one in control this time. But I can see that serves nothing. It only stirred up the resentment and jealousy and…" He trailed off, tears welling in his own eyes.

"Maybe we can start over?" Marleen asked. "From now onwards? I would like to try more to love you, to let you in, and to focus on the future rather than the past."

"Yes, yes, me too," Fernand nodded furiously.

He reached out his arms towards her and, for the first time since they had lived within my walls, I saw Marleen curl into his body and raise her face to kiss her husband.

My gaze drifted elsewhere to allow them their intimacy, and focused on the children, who were now awake and chatting excitedly to their grandparents.

Over the next few months, as Fernand's foot recovered, things continued to change between Marleen and Fernand. She laughed more and gave into his hugs. He in turn was much more carefree in his actions and words. Marleen announced she wanted to go to Polytechnic to study, and Fernand supported this, knowing it was a way to help Marleen focus on her future.

Francia and Mark responded also, giggling and singing, even shouting and running about the house in a way I had never seen. It was as if, through opening her heart to her family, Marleen had opened a door to a life that had previously evaded all of them.

Summer came, and with it warmth both inside and out. The Halden family took trips to 'The Beach', down to Levin to visit her parents, and even rented a cabin in a place called Urenui for the weekend.

Though there were still moments where I could see at times Marleen struggled with her environment and she and Fernand had one or two squabbles, I could also see the effort she was making, and in turn the response she got back from her family and friends was positive and warm.

I understood this. Whenever care and attention was given to me, I felt myself swell with strength and pride. If I was left alone too long, I felt as tired and worn as my lounge-room carpet.

Marleen switched her relief reading job from Awatuna to another school, in the nearby district of Te Kiri. And in the evenings, when Francia and Mark were in bed, she studied using the books the Polytech sent through the mail.

It was still another two years before they had saved the money they needed to move to the city, but the day Fernand and Marleen came back from New Plymouth holding the paperwork for their new home was probably the happiest I had ever seen them.

Fernand whistled and sang German songs as they packed up their belongings and cleaned me from top to bottom, and though I was sad they were leaving, I also felt proud and happy that they had discovered what had been missing from their relationship, right beneath my roof.

Chapter 9

Rhiannon arrived at the beginning of spring, when the wild daffodils were in full bloom, and the mountain was shedding the last of its snowy cloak.

She looked to be about the same age as Joan, and was on her own with her two young daughters, and a trailer full of animals I had not seen before.

Her hair was a tangle of blonde shoulder-length curls falling into her eyes as she wrenched open the trailer door.

"Bobbi! Rowella! Come help me with the goats, please!" She led her animals down the open trailer door, the bells around their collars jingling as they followed Rhiannon and her girls around the back into the garden, where they tethered them to the hedge.

Inside, Rhiannon plonked the daffodils she had picked from the side of the road into an empty bottle, and unpacked from the back of her car pots of herbs and plants, which she sat in the sun on the wash-house windowsill. Rowella and Bobbi both had their mother's tousled hair, but theirs was dark and hung down their backs. They were giggly little girls, with brown eyes and dimples, and a warm golden brown colour to their skin. They danced excitedly through my rooms.

The family did not have much in the way of material things, but I liked the way that Rhiannon decorated over the coming weeks. She stuck up lots of old photos all around the fireplace, and had several sheep skins on the floor, which the girls lazed all over.

Pride of place was an old record player on which they took turns selecting songs to play. Their favourites were The Eagles, Simon and Garfunkel and Fleetwood Mac.

Outside, the goats were tethered to the hedge and were a source of milk, as well as keeping the grass down. Each morning, Rhiannon would go out with a pail and a little wooden stool and sit at the side of either of the two big goats, pulling and coaxing milk from their udders. She would rest her head of curls softly against the goat's side as it chewed peacefully on clover and grass until she was finished.

When Rhiannon came back into the house, the pail would be full of steaming goat's milk, which she poured onto Bobbi and Rowella's porridge as they sat there eying it up hungrily.

About a week after being in the house, Rhiannon came home with a rooster and four chickens, which she housed in a little run made of four-by-two and chicken wire. Within another week of settling in, the chickens were laying eggs and the rooster was climbing up onto the garage roof to wake everyone up with a guttural crow even before the sun had risen.

When their house phone was eventually connected, the little girls sometimes took calls from their father, whom Rhiannon had separated from. She seemed to be on amicable terms with him, but it was very clear that it was well and truly over, and the girls seemed to be accepting of this.

"Sometimes people just don't get on. No matter how much you might be attracted to them, or want to find ways to feel connected. Sometimes, you just can't live with them," Rhiannon divulged to Joan one afternoon (who had quickly become a friend and regular visitor, much to my delight). "Besides, he was pretty bloody useless, if I'm honest!"

Joan's littlest – Louise – was the same age as Rowella, and so the girls often played together while Rhiannon and Joan caught up over coffee. I noticed Joan was pregnant again.

"The last one! He's an unexpected but happy accident," she grinned, patting her tummy.

Rhiannon was very self-sufficient, growing her own vegetables and herbs, and sourcing a lot of the girls' clothes from the secondhand stores in Kaponga and Opunake, but she desperately wanted a job.

"What about David, Joanie? Can he give me a job on the farm? I am happy to do anything!"

And so Joan, being the good friend she was, went back to David to ask him if there were any odd jobs that Rhiannon could do to make some money.

David appeared at the house the following day, standing in the doorway with his boots on.

"Can you drive a tractor?" he asked, shading his eyes from the sun. He wore a wry smile that suggested he didn't believe for a minute Rhiannon would say yes. But she did!

"Drove my Dad's tractor growing up. I think you'll find I'm more than capable," she grinned back.

And so David enlisted Rhiannon as part of the haymaking crew. She would be in charge of driving the tractor and sweep that collected up the bales and deposited them in a pile at the edge of the field, ready to go in the barn.

From my position, I could see two of the haymaking paddocks quite easily, where David's farm bordered on the Barrys'. As well as David and Rhiannon, the crew consisted of David's new worker and Harley, helping out where he could now that he was big enough.

Joan supplied the crew with scones and cups of tea at lunch break, where everyone crowded round under the barn entrance to take shade from the scorching summer sun.

My roof popped and creaked as always, the sun searing on the corrugated iron. It looked like hot work out on the haymaking field.

That night, Rhiannon came in exhausted and sweaty. Bobbi and Rowella, who had been playing down at Joan's with Louise, had already eaten their dinner, so Rhiannon made herself some salad and eggs and sat out on the doorstep in the evening breeze, her bare feet relishing being out of the confines of her gumboots.

"I tell you what," she said to her girls, as they ran around outside under the stars in their pyjamas and bare feet, "tomorrow I am wearing a bloody bikini. It's just way too hot."

When the girls had gone to bed, Rhiannon opened a biscuit tin that she kept up high in the wash-house cupboard and pulled out a glistening green bud that she had picked from one of her herb plants previously.

She sat with her nail scissors and clipped the bud into tiny little pieces, before rolling it up into a piece of rice paper and lighting it. Despite still being out on the doorstep and with many of the windows open to let the cool night air in, the smell from the cigarette she smoked was pungent and earthy.

After a few moments' inhaling deeply on the cigarette, Rhiannon turned her face upwards towards the stars and spent the next half an hour in contemplation, a slight lopsided smile tugging at the corners of her mouth. When she finally got up and turned the lights off and headed to bed, her sleep seemed deep and peaceful.

The next morning, true to her word, Rhiannon dug out a red string bikini top and put it on with her denim cut-off shorts. She pulled on her boots and walked with the girls down the road to meet Joan.

Less than an hour later, I could make out in the distance Rhiannon in the cab of the tractor, driving around the field, sweeping up the bales of hay, her red bikini a beacon amongst the gold fields and the blue of the summer sky. I also watched as David's worker, Trevor, came rumbling up the track in his blue Ford truck, a carpet of dust trailing behind as he drove across to the hay paddock. His head was hanging out the window, his eyes obviously on Rhiannon and her red bikini, and before anyone could warn him to look where he was driving, he had smacked the front of his truck right into a pile of bales, sending them tumbling to the ground.

I could hear David swearing at Trevor at the top of his voice that he better get those bales back into the pile. But I could also hear his deep laughter as he left him to it, Trevor no doubt red-faced at his blatant accident. Rhiannon, meanwhile, was oblivious, or if she had noticed, she pretended not to, from what I could see, continuing to whizz round the field, sweeping up the rectangles that the hay baler left in his wake.

At the end of the week's work, David paid Rhiannon her wages, which she put towards sorting the bills and getting some essentials for the home. And while there were other odd jobs that Rhiannon was able to put her hand to during those summer days, sometimes she just loaded the girls into her rusty old car, along with towels and togs, lunch in Tupperware containers and the car radio turned to full volume, and off they would go, in search of a river, lake, or head to the beach to go swimming.

Rhiannon became firm friends with Joan, with them often looking after each other's children. Joan and Rhiannon were both liberal and open-minded Women who enjoyed the same music, and shared the same fashion sense. Rhiannon was very encouraging of Joan regarding her painting, and was especially passionate about life in general, often igniting debates amongst her and her friends regarding the environment, politics and healthy eating. Rhiannon was a vegetarian, who drank her own goats' milk, tended her chickens' eggs, grew her own veggies and smoked her own type of tobacco. She made no secret of this fact and I wasn't aware she should, until one afternoon, as they sat outside in the garden, Joan pointed out that perhaps Rhiannon shouldn't be smoking "something illegal" so openly.

Rhiannon scoffed.

"I'd much rather smoke pot than tobacco. This is grown by me and is totally natural. Just because the government makes it illegal, doesn't mean it's bad."

She nodded her head at Joan, who was smoking a cigarette. "That's much worse for your baby. You shouldn't do that while you're pregnant." Joan looked down at the store-bought cigarette in her hand, before tossing it at her feet and stubbing it out under her sandal.

The two of them sat in silence, basking in the warmth of the afternoon sun. I stretched slightly, my joints expanding as I made myself comfortable on my foundations.

Joan turned to look at Rhiannon.

"Do you… do you believe in ghosts or spirits?" she asked, her voice slightly hesitant.

"Hmmm… dunno. Why?" Rhiannon's eyes were closed, her arms hung loose by her sides.

"I just… sometimes, when I lived here, I felt like there was a… a presence." Joan let the word hang in the air. Round behind the house the sound of a goat's bell chimed.

"I mean, not a bad one," Joan quickly continued. "I never felt scared or threatened. I just sometimes felt that I wasn't alone, ya know?"

"Do you mean in the house? Or do you mean... the house itself," Rhiannon replied, her eyes still closed. "Cos if you mean a ghost that moves about the house, then no, I don't think there is one here. But... if you mean the house *itself* has a presence, then... yes, I think maybe you are right."

She opened her eyes and sat up in her wicker chair. "Lots of homes have a sense of history, a feeling that they carry from the people that have lived between their walls. Especially if there have been many people." She gestured towards my roof. "And I imagine there have been many people that have lived here."

I listened closely as Rhiannon perfectly described my existence.

"I guess I haven't felt it before in any other place I lived," Joan replied, before adding, "This is a special little house with lots of amazing stories, I'm sure. And I'm glad you sense it too."

Rhiannon and Joan sat and smiled at each other in the sunshine. And, inside my eaves, I smiled too.

Chapter 10

Joan and David, and Rhiannon, were sociable and well-liked members of their community. Not least because they were very active members on the local school board, but also because they threw some of the best house parties. I heard about David's mixtapes and his home-brew beer, dinner parties that ended up in conga lines out in the garden, and Rhiannon had her own as well. Often, hers had only a select few from Awatuna, but she had friends from around the coast, who bought out flagons of beer, and they all sat out in the sunshine with the now-familiar haze of pot smoke hanging in the air.

That summer, when haymaking was finished, Rhiannon decided to throw a party for all the workers to celebrate.

Rhiannon was grateful to David for the work, but often found him a little bossy and self-righteous. He liked to drink and then tell everyone what he thought about things, and Joan and Rhiannon would be constantly telling him to "put a sock in it".

That evening, as they sat outside in the warm summer air, David was being his usual self, postulating over this and that, when Rhiannon had an idea.

"Here, David, have some biscuits. I baked these last night." Rhiannon handed an ice-cream container around, full of biscuits that David and his mates grabbed eagerly.

"Not you, Joanie!" Rhiannon swiped the container from Joan's hands before she could get her fingers around a biscuit. "These are very... fattening." She cast Joan a wink and quickly put the lid on the container before anyone could take any more.

Over the next twenty or so minutes the mood and conversation began to change. David was still talking, but slower now, and his posture began to droop as he settled into his chair.

He and his mates, Neil and Andy, began to find things hilariously funny.

"Shit! I dunno what's come over me, but I feel... weird," Andy said, glancing up at the sky. "The stars are dancing all over the shop!"

"Mate, me too!" David tried to stand up and, as he did so, lost his balance and careened head first into a bush next to the door.

"Woaaaah!" Everyone erupted in a chorus of laughter and whistles, as David stumbled to his feet. He locked eyes on Rhiannon.

"You gave us summin'." He pointed his finger at her. "What was in those biscuits?"

Rhiannon stifled a giggle. "I think you know!"

"Fa fuck's sake, Rhia!" David exclaimed, his eyes red and narrow as he tried to focus. "Joanie, I think I need to go home, love, I don't feel well. I think I'm... stoned, and I don't like it too much."

Joan grabbed his arm, grinning. "Just relax, darling! It's all right if you just go with it."

"Nah, I'm right, thanks. I don't need to go with it." David gestured to the driveway. "Think I'm just gonna walk home." He staggered towards the road, but Joan hurried after him.

"David, I'll drive us!" She steered him towards the car.

"I think you might need to take those two home as well!" Rhiannon gestured towards Neil and Andy, both sitting sleepily in their beach chairs with silly grins on their faces.

Joan rounded up all the men and bundled them into the car. It certainly was a sight, seeing a pregnant Joan backing out of the drive with the three men hanging out the windows shouting their goodbyes, their laughter echoing in the cool night air.

Rhiannon and her daughters lived between my walls for two more years, Rhiannon making most of her living selling goats' milk and the occasional goat.

All of them had names and their own bells, and the Barrys let Rhiannon's animals wander freely in the paddock directly behind the house.

Rhiannon and Joan were now solid friends and they often got together with a couple of other ladies to have a drink and a gossip. I watched with surprise and delight as Joan bought her new baby down to visit. It was not the boy she thought was 'kicking her insides like a goddamn rugby player", but instead another little girl with a shock of dark hair and pudgy white fists. I listened intently as

Joan explained how all the farmers were tipping their milk down the drains in protest that they weren't being paid enough. I was shocked to hear how a tornado had ripped through the south of the province, ripping up trees and tearing through houses, killing a man whose wife and child were only spared because he threw a mattress over them to cover them from debris. I watched in complete awe as Joan sat out in the garden with a sketchbook and pencils, and captured Rhiannon sitting on an old tree stump, hand-feeding her goats. I found myself learning new words and ideas and concepts along with Bobbi and Rowella, as they sat at the kitchen table discussing school work.

Those years flew by and were filled with such happiness and serenity that I didn't want to believe it to be true when Rhiannon announced they were moving.

But move they had to. The flock of goats needed a bigger field, and Rhiannon and her girls all wanted a bigger home. It just so happened that another house in Awatuna, down the Oeo road, was up for rent, so while they were not going far, I knew I would never see them again.

It was a sad day when their photos were taken down from the wall – patches of faded paint the only clue they had ever been there – and boxed away with all their other things.

Just before Rhiannon left, she and the children walked through my rooms one more time to check nothing was left behind.

"Now say goodbye to the house," Rhiannon said, lifting her arms to point at my ceiling.

"Thanks, House!" "Bye, House!" they called, before skipping out the door into the sunshine.

"Goodbye!" I wanted to call back, but the best I could do was a shuddering of my roof.

Rhiannon looked up once again and smiled. "I heard you," she whispered.

She blew me a kiss and shut the door behind her forever.

Chapter 11

The next people who moved in were the Rehunga family, a married couple with three children, and so once again my rooms were filled with the sound of family noises – play fights, games and lots of laughter.

The Rehungas had little money and their children slept on mattresses on the floor, and though the children were outgoing and boisterous, Tamatea and Lorraine Rehunga were quiet, patient parents. Tamatea worked at the timber yard in Opunake, while Lorraine stayed at home and looked after the children.

Their struggle was very real, Lorraine often counting out what money they had on the table, working out how to afford their bills. Every scrap of food was eaten, their veggie garden out back flourishing in the Awatuna weather. Like many of the country children in the district, the Rehunga children all wore hand-me-downs and were often swapping items back and forth. Their personalities shone as they played with local children (including Joan and David's), and they integrated well into their rural life. I watched the eldest three, Huia, Leon and Lydia, as they donned their gumboots and headed to the river through the long moist grass of the back paddock.

I could just see their heads with their haloes of dark hair as they bobbed about, splashing in the river and building dams with rocks and sticks. Their voices carried over the paddock, echoing off the river banks in yelps and screams of laughter. Lorraine, in the meantime, baked and cooked, did washing and pottered about, keeping what little they had sparkling clean.

One afternoon, David came to visit, bringing with him a big, grey, square television that his second eldest son, Luke, helped carry into the house. I couldn't get over how big and tall Luke was now; it was years since I had seen him, and he was now a strapping young man.

They set the TV down on the table as Lorraine and Tamatea hovered about, looking delighted.

"Are you sure I don't owe you anything for it, mate?" Tamatea asked David.

"Nah, mate, she's all yours. We installed our new one last night; so much better − we can get all three channels now!" he proudly replied. "We'll help you get the aerial up now if you like."

The men all went outside, and, propping up a ladder, brought an aerial up onto my roof and installed it next to the chimney.

Next, they ran a lead down the side of my wall and in through a gap in the window, where it was connected to the TV.

After switching it on and moving the aerial around a few times, a picture began to emerge. Fuzzy at first, but in colour, and after a few minutes it began to clear.

"The kids are gonna be so stoked!" Lorraine clapped her hands together with glee. "Our first colour TV − and look how big it is! Thank you so much, David!" She

112

turned and gave David a big toothy grin, which he reciprocated.

That night, as the family sat round the dinner table, the children squirmed impatiently, shovelling their food into their mouths with excited anticipation.

When they were finally excused to leave the table, on came the television and all three sat in a semicircle, soft happy grins imprinted on their faces.

I watched the television with them, learning more about the world with each nature programme or documentary that came on. There was also some drama and comedy, which would have the whole family crying or laughing, depending on the topic. I was intrigued by the television, especially when one programme talked about 'The Beach'.

Suddenly, pictures flashed up, and there it was. Instead of fields of grass, as I was used to, I was witness to fields of grey sand, rocks, pools of water, and, of course, the ocean.

Waves ebbed and flowed, crashing on the sand in white foamy ridges. People frolicked in the water, rode their surfboards as Joanie once did, and lay in the warmth of the sun on the sand.

To me, it looked like an amazing place to visit, and I could finally grasp the allure of the beach that had often taken my inhabitants off for a visit. I also realised now that it was the ocean that I could just make out in the far distance, the line of deep blue that met the sky. 'The horizon', as I now understood it to be called.

Another thing that was paid close attention to on the TV was the news and the weather. This was most helpful to me, as I was able to anticipate the wind or rain coming and prepare myself accordingly. One night, the weather lady told us of approaching high winds and rain, and so I nestled down into my foundations (trying not to make too much noise) and held tight.

The wind and rain did indeed come that night, and, try as it might to batter my roof off, it was unsuccessful. The following day, the family were warm and cosy within my walls having their Sunday lunch as the wind whipped round the garden outside, ripping the heads off flowers, and picking up leaves that slapped and clung to the window pane like moths.

I heard a rumble in the distance and saw a lorry approaching from the East. It was going quite fast, as cars and trucks often did along this straight piece of road, but the wind was equally fast and strong. I watched as the lorry lost control, skidded on the wet road and suddenly it was on its side, the front windscreen cracking and the back door of the lorry flying open, its contents spilling all over the tarseal and even onto my driveway.

"What the hell was that?" exclaimed Tamatea, standing up so fast he knocked his water all over the table.

Everyone stopped eating, knives and forks poised at open mouths.

"Sounded like a car crash?" Lorraine also got to her feet and rushed to the front door, followed by the family.

They piled out onto the driveway and, quickly assessing the accident, Tamatea turned to the children.

"Get inside now!" They did as they were told and turned on their heels, pushing against the wind.

Tamatea and Lorraine rushed over to the lorry's cab, where the male driver was inside.

I watched as they helped pull him from the wreckage, Tamatea having to reach right inside and haul him out. He seemed okay, apart from a few chipped teeth that he spat from his bloodied mouth.

"You need an ambulance, mate?" Tamatea yelled above the wind, as they helped him over to the front door.

"Ahh, I think I'm okay, but might pay to call one, I suppose," he replied, slightly limping as they all came inside.

The children all watched wide-eyed as the stranger sat down in their lounge, blood stains on his t-shirt, while their Mum grabbed a blanket off the bed and wrapped it around his shoulders.

"I'll get the neighbour to bring his tractor and clear it off the road, okay, mate? Won't take long." Tamatea began pulling on his boots again, while Lorraine picked up the phone to call an ambulance and then called to see if David could come with his tractor.

"All the produce is all over the road!" the driver called after him. "We probably can't sell that now − you may as well take what you can." He threw Tamatea a tooth-chipped smile.

Tamatea nodded approvingly.

"Righto, then, Huia and Leon, you come with me."

They headed back out into the storm, and while David came with his tractor and towed the lorry to the side out of the way of passing motorists, who slowed down to rubberneck the accident, Tamatea and the children ran out with boxes and began picking up the produce that had spilled onto the road.

The lorry had been laden with dairy products, so they filled their boxes with everything from ice cream and chocolate milk, to yoghurt and blocks of cheese.

Once David had moved the lorry, he also helped gather up what remained of the produce.

Items had flown into the ditch on the side of the road, so they were pulling out blocks of cheese that, though covered in muddy water, were perfectly edible due to their plastic casings.

"Woah, kids, we're gonna feast like kings on all this!" Tamatea exclaimed.

Both boxes were full to the brim, so Tamatea had to go get a plastic bag to keep the rest of the damaged goods in. David also got himself a haul to take back to his family.

Later on, when the ambulance had been to collect the lorry driver and take him out to the doctor in Opunake, a recovery vehicle arrived with big flashing lights to pull the lorry onto its trailer. The children were allowed to watch this part, and stood excitedly in their little raincoats and boots, watching as the truck rescued the lorry and headed off back to the coast.

"What an exciting day!" Lorraine exclaimed, mopping up the spilled water and clearing the table.

"Jeez, I'll say!" Tamatea flopped down onto the sofa. "I feel bad for the driver; he lost the company a fair amount of stock today! But I guess they'll be insured, and he's lucky he wasn't hurt worse."

The children sat quietly now, overwhelmed by the day's event. The wind had died down eventually, but the rain still fell, dancing its militant steps on my corrugated roof.

Then Lydia's little voice piped up.

"Does this mean we might be able to have dessert tonight?" She nodded towards the now fully stocked fridge, her green eyes beaming hopefully.

Tamatea laughed and reached out to pull his daughter in for a hug.

"Yes it does, wee one, yes it does!"

Chapter 12

The Rehungas only stayed for two years in total. It seemed to be a familiar scenario that I became used to – people living within my walls for a few short years and then leaving. But once Lydia started school, Lorraine was able to get a job at the supermarket out in Opunake, so it made sense for them to move out there.

I missed that rag-tag little family and hoped things were now easier for them.

While I had been kept clean by Lorraine, I was definitely showing my age; signs of wear and tear were everywhere.

Despite this, the Barry family decided to sell me as I was, and I was worried for a short time over who would own me now.

So it was to my absolute delight when David and Joanie pulled up and unlocked my front door.

"Hi, House!" Joan called, sweeping through my rooms and opening the windows with gusto.

Another car, an old green Holden, pulled up behind their Fairmont and out got their son Luke!

I soon learned that there had been a dairy boom and David had bought the adjoining farm from Jack and Ruth. This included me, and so I was to now be home to Luke, who, at eighteen, was a grown man and needed to live on his own. He had been taken on by one of the neighbours down the Oeo road to help with the farm, milking cows and learning the ropes.

As Harley lived in New Plymouth and had no interest in being on the farm, it – and maybe Me – would all be Luke's one day. Jack and Ruth, who were now ready to retire, were going to be moving into Opunake, into what Joan called 'a new build'.

While Luke was a farm-savvy, hardworking young man, he didn't know the first thing about keeping a house. Despite Joan trying to educate him on all things domestic, Luke wasn't having it. He preferred his Mum to stay out of his business, and that included stepping foot over my threshold.

I watched in amusement as Luke attempted to boil some potatoes, but got so caught up in watching the cricket that they boiled dry. The bottom of the pot began to burn and smoke, and so the whole lot – burnt potatoes and blackened saucepan – got thrown out under the hedge.

Another time, he attempted to wash his sheets in the secondhand top loader that now resided in the wash-house. However, Luke failed to notice the pair of red underpants that were caught up in the sheets, and, much to his dismay, when he pulled out the washing, the sheets were now a shade of pale pink! Luke was furious and swore black and blue, annoyed with himself that he had not paid more attention to his mother's instructions.

His first year living beneath my roof was one of trial and error as he learned the ways of living independently.

That's not to say that he didn't still go up to David and Joan's and have dinner; he was there most Sundays for a roast, and sometimes took his washing with him as well.

Luke loved music and had what he called a 'Boom Box', which he played all his favourite tapes on. He constantly had U2 on repeat as well as INXS, Australian Crawl, Split Endz and Men At Work. I came to know all their songs, and sometimes I would find myself singing the chorus to a song in my mind, even when Luke didn't have the music on! Luke was also very social and had quite a few friends who would stop by for a beer, to share some fish and chips and talk about future plans. One idea they often threw around was of going travelling to Australia.

I knew by now that there were towns and cities, other provinces and whole other countries out there in the world, even places where people spoke different languages such as Fernand had often used. I was also aware that Australia was one of New Zealand's closest neighbours. Television gave me some sort of perspective of distance, but the idea of leaving one shore and travelling to another was beyond me. Yet, it was a concept that excited much conversation and imaginings amongst Luke and his friends.

Luke planned to go travelling after another year working, but he never really mentioned this whenever his girlfriend Tina was around. Luke and Tina were madly in love, and Luke, especially, was besotted.

Tina was from a town about twenty-five minutes' drive away to the East, from a good, solid family, and she had ambitions of being a dancer. She was tall and beautiful-looking, with long sandy hair and a smattering of freckles across the bridge of her nose. She came to stay with Luke regularly, and some days the two of them would spend the whole day in bed, wrapped up in each other's arms, talking for hours or dozing peacefully.

On Sundays, Luke had rugby, so the two of them would cuddle up on the bench seat of his Holden and hoon off at speed to Opunake. While Luke wasn't a huge fan of the theatre, he would often put on his best jeans and shirt to go and watch Tina perform, as she danced professionally at various shows around the province.

One day, when the two of them were entwined in Luke's pale pink sheets, slightly hungover from a party they had been to the night before, Luke declared that he would love Tina forever.

Tina smiled and furrowed her brow.

"Even when I'm a famous dancer?"

Luke stroked her forehead with the tip of his finger.

"Of course, even when you're famous. I'll be there for you whatever you do, babe. I promise."

"Even if my dancing takes me all across the world?" Tina twisted her head so she could see Luke's face properly.

"If I can come too sometimes, and watch you perform, and make sure no other fella gets his mitts on you – then yeah, sure, all around the world!" He gave her a playful poke in the ribs, which made her squeal with laughter.

I smiled to myself and let my thoughts and gaze wander elsewhere so they could have their privacy.

Their love was unlike any I had experienced under my roof before. This was young love, I realised. The kind of love that makes you want to forego everything else and just give over to the overwhelming feelings you have. I knew that I would never be able to experience that kind of Human love myself, but I understood it. I saw how it could consume you, fulfil you, and eventually, if you let it – destroy you.

One day, when Tina and Luke were enjoying fish and chip takeaways and a video, Luke's phone rang. It was Tina's Mum wanting to speak with her.

After a few minutes of conversation, Tina excitedly turned to Luke and mouthed, "I got in!"

She talked for a few minutes more and then hung up, spinning on her toes in delight.

"I made it, baby! I made it to the provincial finals! I'm gonna be dancing in New Plymouth next week in hope of making it to the Nationals!"

Luke jumped up and bundled her in his arms.

"That's amazing! Well done. Of course you made it, you're the best in the province!"

"Will you come watch me?"

Luke looked at her with eyes full of love.

"Of course I will come watch you. You couldn't keep me away!"

The two of them kissed and hugged some more, before Luke swept Tina up into his arms and carried her into the bedroom, where he kicked the door closed behind him.

Tina won the provincial finals, and from here it was time to dance in the New Zealand Championship.

She would be representing Taranaki amongst many other girls in the country and it was going to be on television.

Luke was beside himself with excitement, telling anyone who visited that his "Missus is gonna be on the telly". I felt excited for them both too, but with so much preparation for Tina, and so much farm work to be done, Luke was often alone leading up to the competition.

However, he was determined to go and watch her perform, so David gave him two days off work so he could join her in Auckland.

The week before the competition, Luke called Tina for his usual evening conversation.

I could tell it didn't go as he planned. It sounded like Tina didn't want Luke to come to the competition now because he might distract her.

Despite Luke's protests and explaining he'd even gotten two days off, it appeared Tina was set in her decision. When he hung up the phone, he was visibly deflated.

"Fuck's sake!" he cursed, kicking the foot stool across the room.

I watched him as he stood there in the middle of the room, turning his thoughts over in his mind. Then he reached for the phone on the wall again and, turning the dial, called up David to tell him he would be making it to milking that weekend after all.

Even though Tina had told Luke he couldn't come to the competition, after speaking with his Dad, he resigned himself to accepting her decision, and instead decided to be as supportive as he could. It appeared Luke was learning the ways of love and relationships, and that meant sometimes things not working out as first anticipated.

He still called and wished her luck, and even sent a big bouquet of flowers out to her parents.

And when the weekend of the televised competition came round, Luke was so nervous for her he couldn't bear to watch the programme with anyone else, instead pitching up in front of the TV with a few cans of beer and a takeaway.

The television show appeared to be quite prestigious, with a big seated audience and presented by one of the more well-known entertainers of the time.

Each dancer came out and performed their piece, and then were judged by a panel of people who were representatives from the world of dance.

I watched and waited alongside Luke, as each dancer came and went, excited to see what my part-time inhabitant, Tina, might do.

At last it was her turn, as the announcer's voice boomed into the microphone.

"And representing Taranaki, please put your hands together for Miss Tina Hornby!"

The music began, softly at first, and out came Tina, a show of smiles and open arms.

The first thing I noticed was how different she looked with a lot of make-up on, her hair slicked back, and in an outfit I was unfamiliar with, cascading all around her.

Luke sat upright, a nervous smile on his face, as he watched his girlfriend gracefully arch and jump. She moved about the stage with ease and confidence, and I was enchanted to watch someone I knew dance inside the grey, glass box.

Suddenly, Tina went to spin on her toes, but, as she did, she slipped slightly. The smile on Tina's face became one of anxiety, as it was obvious the slip had rattled her. Tina couldn't remember the next step!

She stopped in her tracks while the music continued, her eyes searching the eaves above her, as if the theatre's heavens could provide the answer.

"Come on, girl!" Luke leaned forward at the TV, willing his girlfriend to remember. "Just make something up!"

Tina suddenly remembered what was supposed to happen next, and quickly leapt into action to try and get her routine back on track; but, as she was now behind, it meant the music finished before her routine was supposed to. Tina came out of her last turn before she had completed it properly and bowed into her final position.

While the crowd still clapped and cheered, and Tina smiled away at the audience and the camera, as she left the stage I could see her face crumple.

"Ah fuck, poor girl. But at least she carried on and finished it!" Luke said to himself. He drained the last of the beer, and got up to use the bathroom.

When he came back, the judges' scores were being announced for Tina's performance.

"Well, that's that then." Luke shook his head as Tina's scores were read out – too low to even put her in the final ten.

He got up to switch off the TV and, as he did so, the phone on the wall jingled.

It was Joan on the other end, wanting to talk about the performance.

"Yeah... yeah, I know, Mum... Yeah, I will make sure I do... okay... bye."

Luke headed into his bedroom and lay down on the bed, pulling the blanket up around his shoulders. He reached for the pillow that Tina usually lay on, and pressed his face into it so he could breathe in her scent. Within a few minutes he was fast asleep, his face relaxed and at peace.

Luke woke in the morning to the sound of the phone on the wall ringing again.

It was Tina. She wanted to see him as soon as she got back from Auckland, which would be that evening.

Luke offered to pick her up from the airport after milking, and despite Tina's poor performance and result, Luke was thrilled to be seeing her again after two weeks apart.

He came charging in through my front door, kicking off his grubby boots into the wash-house, and ran himself a bath. He shaved his face, and dabbed on some cologne, and smiled at his reflection in the mirror as he pulled on a clean t-shirt.

He was gone for about two hours, so I assumed perhaps they had stopped somewhere to get dinner, but when he walked in the door, Luke was alone. His face looked streaked with tears, his eyes red and swollen.

I wondered what could have possibly happened.

Luke picked up the phone and dialled his parents' number.

"Mum?... It's me. Can you c...c...come down here, please?... Tina's d...d...dumped me!" Luke let out a sob as he said the last words, and placed the phone back on the wall cradle. His head hung to his chest, tears coming steadily now, dripping down his handsome nose and onto the floor.

Within a few minutes, Joan arrived and rushed straight over to give him a hug.

"What's happened, darling?" She placed her hand under his chin and tipped up his face so she could search his eyes. "What did she say?"

"She said that after the weekend and what happened at the competition, she needed to make some serious decisions. She said her teacher told her that if she truly wants to make it as a dancer then she needs to get rid of any... *distractions*." Luke spat the last word out as if it were a bitter taste on his tongue. "Then she said that being a successful dancer would require her going places, places that I wouldn't be able to go, and that being on the

127

farm with me was preventing her from doing that. So, basically, what she's saying is, I'm holding her back!"

Joan frowned in angst for her son.

"Oh, darling, I'm so sorry to hear this, but you know this isn't your fault, don't you? You didn't muck up Tina's dance; she did that herself. It's not nice to hear them say those things, but I guess maybe I can see their point, what with all the time she does spend here…" Joan's voiced trailed off as Luke turned to her, his face a red angry twist.

"Are you taking their side?"

"No, no, of course not, it's not about taking sides. I'm just saying that perhaps they have a point, in that Tina is here a lot, and dancing requires a huge amount of discipline and time."

Her voice took on a pleading quality as Joan realised her son was probably hurting too much to see sense, and I felt his frustration within every inch of my being.

"I don't care, Mum! I love her! I promised her I would never leave her, and she's just thrown me aside like I'm… like I'm fucking nothing!"

Luke's tears began again, rushing down his cheeks, encouraging his nose to run.

Joan tried to pull him in for a hug, but Luke shrugged her off.

"Just go, Mum. I want to be alone."

"Luke…"

"Just GO!" Luke shouted, the pain and anger he felt directed into the face of his dear mother.

Joan pursed her lips and nodded in resignation.

"Okay, darling, I'm going. But we're here for you, OK? If you want Dad or me, we're right here."

She headed out the door, her own eyes moist in sympathy.

Luke sat down on the sofa and buried his face into one of the old hand-me-down cushions that Joan had sewn.

He began to cry again, long guttural sobs that wracked his chest and choked his throat. Luke rocked back and forth, the cushion pressed against his face as he exhausted himself to the point of sleep. I watched his face, now relaxed and peaceful, as his dreams carried him from the reality of his heartbreak. I continued to watch him as, over the next few weeks, he ebbed between utter despair and sadness – to anger and frustration.

He called up Tina and begged her to change her mind, crying down the phone until Tina's Mum or Dad took the phone and tried to console him. In the end they asked Luke to stop calling altogether as he was being selfish now, not allowing Tina to move on and focus on her career.

He got drunk and stoned, and watched TV until the early hours of the morning, when there was nothing more to watch but a black and white fuzzy haze that swam in front of his eyes.

He barely ate, simply forgetting to, and became exhausted, coming home from milking and falling straight into bed, and, as a result, Luke allowed my rooms to become untidy and dirty.

I wished there was something I could do or say to let him know he was not alone, or to offer some comfort. But this was the difficulty I faced in being neither 'here' nor 'there'.

I was a part of this reality and yet only in a way where I was an observer, rather than a participant. I felt every emotion, soaked up every conversation, experienced every relationship, and allowed it all to imbue my walls and floors 'till I was soaked in stories and history and hope. Yet I was forever burdened with the inability to truly communicate with my inhabitants, often surrounded by people, yet isolated in my very existence. Once again, I found myself wondering if there were any other houses out there like me, who were going through a similar experience. I very much doubted this and tried hard not to dwell on the idea. Not because I thought I was particularly special or unique, but quite the opposite. If there *were* others like me, I would never know them. That, for the rest of my days, I would continue to only live through those who existed between my walls. Those who never saw me, or heard me, or knew me. Forever balanced in this in-between world until my wooden limbs crumbled to dust, my lonely soul caught on a breeze, and I would be sent spiralling up into the cold evening air.

Luke seemed unable to shake off the pain of his broken heart. It was as if the conversation he had had with Tina around their break-up had shattered his confidence, and was making him second-guess himself. I felt like my walls were no longer offering him comfort or protection, but instead, the more time he spent within me, getting stoned and watching TV, the more his spirit was being confined. I was too small for Luke, even as a single man; he needed to be somewhere where he could see the merit of his worth again. To spread his wings, to open his heart.

In the end, it was David who decided enough was enough. He knew that Luke wasn't being as proactive as he usually was in doing his job on the farm, and so one evening he came in after milking to have a talk with his son. He told Luke that, by staying put, he was only making it harder for himself, as most of his memories here were of him and Tina. That by clinging to those memories he was allowing his energy to be sucked dry. This, in turn, was affecting his work, his friendships, and his communication with his parents. He also explained it in practical terms as well. David needed to make more money and Luke barely paid a cent in rent. It would benefit everyone if he moved out and found a new place to live. Somewhere closer to town, perhaps; somewhere where he could start afresh. Then, next year, perhaps he could look into going to Australia to work, just as he had always planned to.

At first, Luke protested that he wasn't ready to move, but after a bit more encouragement, he finally relented.

Two weeks later, he found somewhere new to live, another farm cottage, but one that was apparently bigger, brighter, up on a hill and closer to Opunake.

Again, I watched as boxes were packed up, pictures brought down from my walls, floors swept and cupboards cleaned. Joan and her girls did most of the work, trying to ease the pain for Luke as his life shrunk down to a mere trailer-load of things.

To begin with, Luke was slow in sorting things out and making any progress of his own, but after he found a photo of Tina in the drawer pressed between two old Christmas cards, Luke's pace quickened. In one weekend, the traces of his life beneath my roof were wiped clean with a damp cloth, folded and packed into cases and boxes, and, just like that – gone.

I had to admit I felt relieved to be free of Luke's anxiety and sadness. But I also felt restless and envious that he was able to just pack up and leave.

Though I knew I was supposed to be resigned to my fate, here on the Eltham Road, I couldn't help but cast my gaze out West, to hold onto the shimmering sliver of silver I saw in the distance, long after the earth had turned on its side and the night cast its cloak over my eyes.

Chapter 13

Of all the people who had come and gone throughout the many eras that I existed in Awatuna, I had always felt some sort of attachment to them in one way or another. Whether it was through the conversations that were exchanged, the relationships that grew and flourished, or just the nature of the way they did things, there had always been a connection between myself and my inhabitants.

So it was the strangest thing to feel absolutely no connection whatsoever to the next people that rented me from David and Joan.

After sitting idle for what seemed like another year, and having no interest from any potential renters, I guess David was relieved to find anyone willing to rent my now rather shoddy rooms.

The inhabitants were two men who went by the names Hast and Wally. They rode motorbikes and worked at a factory. Neither of them spent much time at home, their jobs starting early enough to have them out on the road just as the sun was creeping over the windowsill.

When they did come home, there was never much conversation between the two of them; it was usually a shower, and straight to bed. I figured they must eat out somewhere, perhaps at the pub, as neither of them ever cooked anything in my kitchen. They often seemed slightly inebriated when they trundled in the front door, though obviously not enough to prevent them from ripping into the drive, their motorbikes roaring furiously. Cleanliness was also not a high priority, with most of my rooms gathering dust and dead flies at an alarming rate, and the shower and toilet becoming stained in rings of grime.

Their routine of coming and going went on for about two months, and, while I tried to find something to connect me to these inhabitants, there was nothing about them that I could find to help me do so. They had no personal items other than some toiletries and clothes, and a few magazines lying around. They didn't own a TV, and my cupboards lay bare. I listened to their conversations, but they consisted only of talk about 'the factory', meeting some of the other guys at the pub, or going to a party. I felt confused by this sense of isolation, whilst still having people effectively living between my walls. In the past, I always felt something for my inhabitants. I would try to keep them safe and warm, and they in return gave their energy through their actions, conversations or stories. I soon came to realise that the reason I felt no connection with Hast or Wally was simply because they felt nothing for me. I was merely a stopping point in the cycle of their daily lives, somewhere to sleep and wash, but not much more. I wasn't considered to be their home; they didn't treat me as one, and this could not have been made more evident by what was to unfold the following Friday night.

The day started out as usual, Hast and Wally out the door by 7am, hooning off on their motorbikes and leaving me in solitude.

However, at around six o'clock, it wasn't just their bikes that turned into my driveway. Several other bikes and riders pulled up, followed by a few cars.

People came flooding into my front room, their heavy boots and loud voices reverberating around the house: women with frizzy teased-out hair, too much make-up and high-pitched laughter, men with cigarettes hanging out their mouths as they cracked the rings on their beer cans.

Someone had brought along a portable stereo system, which they cranked to full volume. It wasn't music I had heard before, but it was loud and harsh, and disconcerting for my old walls. Don't get me wrong, I had been witness to plenty of parties beneath my roof before – Rhiannon had her fair share, as had Luke, but theirs had been different. The 'vibe', as Rhiannon used to say, had been different.

I couldn't put my metaphorical finger on it – but the energy on this night felt edgy and slightly noxious. I tried to drift away from taking in what was happening, people stumbling and shouting, and swilling beer all over the carpet. One guy fell against the bedroom door and knocked it clean off one of its hinges.

I cringed with every cigarette that missed its beer can and instead fell into a pile of ash on the floor or table. Yet every time I tried to cast my gaze away out towards the stars, or focus on the cool night air edging under my eaves, I couldn't. I was continuously knocked back into consciousness by a shout, or raucous laughter, or something smashing on the floor.

There was an altercation in my kitchen between two of Wally's mates: they were arguing over money, one obviously owing the other, and it was becoming heated. Wally just looked on, a lopsided grin on his face as he watched them square-up.

In the corner of my lounge, a woman and two men were chatting, and, as I now turned my attention to them, I realised that the woman was actually quite young, probably early twenties, and looking increasingly uncomfortable with the conversation.

One of the men reached out and placed a hand on her bare shoulder. He let it slide down around her back, where he gave her bottom an aggressive 'pat' and pulled her towards him. The other guy just laughed and muttered something under his breath I couldn't catch.

She laughed slightly, her bloodshot eyes darting nervously back and forth between the men.

Suddenly, the voices from the kitchen became raised as the argument boiled over into a full-blown fight. Punches were thrown and some of the other men tried to intervene and pull them apart, which seemed to only make it worse. One of Wally's mates now had a bloody nose, and when he pulled his hand away and saw the blood, it sent him into a crazed rage.

I was suddenly reminded of when Carl and Amy had lived here: the violence and the fear, the uncertainty of what next. And what happened next was just as horrible. While the fight was going on in the kitchen, the two men who had backed the young woman into the corner of the lounge now pulled her into the bedroom. One of them was kissing her neck, his hand locked against the back of her head, while the other man began to unbuckle his belt.

"No... no – I don't want to do this!" She pulled back as hard as she could to release herself from the grip of the first man. In doing so, she fell back against the bed.

"Too late, love, it's happening now!" he growled, and pounced on her, holding her down.

"Come on, Pete, give me a hand, would ya!"

"No! Get off me!" The girl pushed and kicked as the first man tried to restrain her, struggling between putting his hand over her mouth and trying to stop her legs from kicking.

The second man moved forward at speed now, pulling up her dress and ripping down her underwear. He finally got his belt off and I realised in horror that this poor girl was about to get raped beneath my roof while a fight went on in the kitchen.

I panicked, wondering what I could do to stop this from happening. The men were still trying to hold the girl down, almost enjoying the struggle, as she was surely exhausting herself. They took turns taunting her, telling her what they were going to do to her, groping her breasts and between her legs, before flipping her onto her stomach. Meanwhile, the fight in the kitchen involved several people now who were taking turns holding the men back from one another and trying to calm the situation. No one was focused on the bedroom, and as long as the girl had her mouth covered, there was no reason for anyone to be.

I knew that what I was about to do would cause some damage to my structure and potentially to some of the people in the house, but I didn't care. I had to do what I could to prevent the situation in the bedroom from going any further and help that poor girl.

I began to shake my walls as hard as I could, trying to replicate what I had felt each time there had been an earthquake. I banged my roof up and down, and with each jolt felt the windows shudder, the frames grinding against each other. The two men stopped what they were doing and looked at one another, and the voices in the kitchen quickly died down.

"Earthquake!" someone exclaimed.

I realised that this was not going to be enough, though, as the men in the bedroom only moved with greater haste.

"I'm gonna get it in this bitch – earthquake or not!" Pete grabbed hold of the back of the girl's ankles and yanked them towards his now-naked crotch.

With that one movement, I shook my roof and walls with as much strength as I could muster, pushing down onto my foundations with all the energy I had left in my tired old bones.

Suddenly, to my own surprise and certainly of everyone inside – the windows in the bedroom exploded.

Glass shattered and flew into the bedroom, covering the men and hitting them in their faces.

Both of them fell to the floor, yelling in pain and clutching at their eyes, releasing the girl, who now began to scream and scream. I kept going.

Now, not only the bedroom but the lounge windows shattered as well. Glass exploded into the lounge, sending people flying out the door or onto the floor.

"GET OUUUUUUUUUUUT!!!!!!!!!" I screamed, giving my roof one final jolt, sending the top of the chimney crumbling onto the ground again.

People in the house screamed in fear at this 'earthquake', unlike anything they had heard or felt before, fleeing out into the night air, grabbing their keys out of their pockets and starting their bikes and cars with such speed, some of them nearly crashed into one another.

The girl in the bedroom jumped up now, pulling down her dress, sobbing hysterically, still in part fear, but also what seemed part relief, as she made her escape.

I watched as she dashed out the door along with everyone else, but instead of getting into a car or onto a bike, she began to run up the road towards David and Joanie's.

That's when I finally stopped my shaking.

The two men in the bedroom, their faces covered in blood, stumbled out into the lounge, almost colliding with Hast, who was heading towards them.

"What the fuck just happened?" one of them shouted, but Hast didn't hear him. He grabbed a bag out from under the bed and threw everything he had in the room into it, packing as quickly as he could, his face ashen in fear.

Wally was in the sunroom doing the same thing, but yelled back at the men, "Get the fuck outta here, Faulks! We're leaving, and so should you!"

Within ten minutes, the whole place was empty; Wally and Hast had their bags on their backs and roared out of my driveway, leaving the lights on and the front door open.

In the far distance, I could hear a police siren wailing, coming from the East, but the gang of bikes and cars was now heading towards Opunake. Another car was coming down the road at speed, but everyone had gone by the time David pulled in, his tyres skidding and throwing up gravel. He got out of the car, disbelief etched all over his face, as he took in my broken windows, my broken chimney top and loose corrugated roof.

"What the bloody hell happened here...?" He began to walk towards my front door, just as the police car from Kaponga pulled into the drive.

The two officers joined David in looking utterly confused and shocked.

"It's like there's been an earthquake... but only in this house," said one.

"More like a bomb's gone off!" the other replied.

The three men walked around my rooms, absolutely baffled. I heard David giving his account to the policemen, telling them that he had been in bed almost asleep when he heard banging and a girl screaming at the back door. He had told Joan to lock the front door quickly, as he initially thought perhaps it was burglars trying to create a distraction at the back door and come in through the front.

But when he finally opened the back door, there stood a girl shivering and crying.

"Help me!" she had said, practically falling into the laundry. "Some men tried to rape me at a party down the road!"

David and Joan had immediately called the police, and while Joan comforted the girl, David had set off down the road to confront the men, his shotgun lying across the passenger seat.

However, he didn't need it. As the girl later explained to the police when they brought her back down the road to get her to show them what had happened and where, she told them the 'earthquake' had scared everyone off, that it had made the windows explode, and there had been a long, loud scream, "Like a train throwing on its brakes, or a plane about to crash... and it sounded like it said something."

The officers had looked at each other, a glance that said, "She's obviously in shock."

But David leaned in when she said this, his eyebrows narrowing.

"It sounded like it *said* something? What did *it* say?"

The girl wiped her nose and looked at David as if she could barely believe it herself.

"It said... 'Get out'... Only... it said it like it was really, really angry."

David gave a strange little half-smile and turned his eyes up towards my ceiling.

"And you think... maybe... this earthquake... it stopped you from being raped?"

"I know it sounds crazy, but if that hadn't happened... I can't even bear to think what else might have." She wrapped her arms around herself, her tiny frame swamped by David's big wool jacket that Joan had given her.

Again, David leaned in. This time he smiled at the girl and said very quietly, almost in a whisper –

"It's okay. I believe you, as crazy as it is – I actually do."

One of the officers was taking notes; the other looked around my lounge warily, as if expecting a ghost to jump out.

I felt like saying, "It's all right, I'm not haunted – it's just me – the house!" But I knew I would need to be quiet from here on in. I had done all I needed to do.

The glass was repaired in my windows over the following days, and two big heavy deadbolts affixed to my front door. David was taking no chances: he didn't want anyone coming and squatting within my rooms, and Hast and Wally were not welcome after the damage they had caused... well, the damage they had helped cause.

But he needn't have worried. I knew none of the people who had been at the party that night would be returning. I had made sure of that.

The police had said they would be following up the girl's claim and that they would also try to sort out Hast and Wally for damages, but I never knew what happened because, apart from my windows being replaced and the bolts added to the door, no one came to see me again for a while.

Once again, I surveyed the damage to my walls, floor and roof. I was a wreck. I looked like it and felt like it, and I didn't even want to think about what would happen next.

The sun sat low on the horizon, filling my rooms with a soft golden glow that bounced from wall to wall. But even the caress of its rays could not warm the cold, hard feeling that seeped throughout my structure. I felt sad. Alone. 'Depressed' was a word I had once heard Luke use.

I imagined a giant thumb pressing down on my roof from above, squashing my light, cracking my paintwork, my walls caving in slightly at the weight.

I did the only thing I knew how to do at times like this: I turned my gaze outwards towards the mountain, the trees, out over the fields, and always West. Always to the silvery sliver of light that rested between the sky and the ocean. The horizon. I looked, and watched, and waited.

Chapter 14

I heard the bolts to the front door being jiggled and unlocked, and pulled myself out of a hazy slumber. It was David and Joan! I wasn't sure how long I had been alone; sometimes days would pass, weeks, even months, when I went into my hibernation state.

The sun was up and it felt very warm, as if summer had finally laid her soothing hand across my cold iron roof. My limbs started to pop and expand in the heat.

"Yes, yes, nice to see you too, house!" Joan laughed, pushing her way into my dusty lounge room, holding a long-handled broom, bucket and cloth.

The two of them spent the next few hours sweeping out my rooms, my windows wide open to the soft summery breeze. Dust and ash, rubbish and bits of glass were swept up and taken outside. David began the arduous task of ripping up my old matted carpet, sweat gathering at his brow as he tugged and pulled at its edges, before finally getting it rolled up and dumped out on the drive.

I was slightly excited now. I thought that the only thing that could be happening was another family was perhaps moving in. At the same time, I felt tentative and worried.

I wasn't sure what I could handle any more. The idea of a large family made me feel intimidated and wearisome, but the thought of just one person living here wasn't so nice either.

I had never really thought about it until that moment, but I realised I resented the fact that I could never choose my inhabitants. They came and went as they pleased and did what they liked within my walls, and I was powerless to say or do anything about it... for the most part, anyway.

I shuddered slightly, unable to contain my frustration.

"God, it just feels like the walls might come down any minute," Joan called out to David. "It's definitely time for her to go!" She stood up, hands on hips, and looked around, shaking her head.

"Yep, and it will free up a heap of space in this paddock once it's gone, too!" David called back. "I'm looking forward to knocking down that garage, too − we can use those breeze blocks on the new shed!"

Suddenly it dawned on me. I was not about to get another family. Not even a single farm worker.

I was being cleaned out because I was going to be dismantled. Destroyed. Taken off the plot and probably to some wood yard where my limbs would be turned into garden chips.

I felt a wash of emotions rush over me. Of course they would want to get rid of me. I had been here for decades! I was old, tired, and worn out. My time here on this farm in Awatuna was now done, and in a way I knew

I should not have expected that I would or could live on forever. I was only a little white cottage, after all.

However, I had never thought this far ahead... I had never envisioned that this day might actually come.

The following week, some men came and looked at me. They wrote things down and seemed to be measuring and making calculations. I gathered that this was to work out what to save and what to discard; however, I didn't really want to know the details. I shut down my gaze and focused my thoughts inwards, blocking out their conversations.

Not long after, my electricity and plumbing were disconnected. The beds were thrown out, and the bath was dragged out onto the back of a truck by David and a couple of mates, to be sold at a reclamation yard.

I felt immense sadness, knowing that I would never experience anyone else living beneath my roof. No more stories to bear witness to, memories to make or things to learn.

I thought of all the people who had lived within my embrace, and the emotions they had expressed that had unconsciously permeated every inch of my being. I may not be 'alive' in the Human sense of the word, but I was very much alive because of the energy that had seeped through my walls, my floor, my ceiling, as if the breath of others within my rooms had breathed life into my very soul.

Now, all of that was to be taken away.

For most of my 'life' I had lived in the present moment. Never knowing (or having control of) what was to happen next – or who was going to walk through my door – meant that I could never have any expectations or hopes beyond what I already knew and had experienced.

When I had tried to piece together the 'before' time from the fragments of memory that I did have, things had never quite come together. I knew that I had not always been this house… but, being what I was here and now was all that made absolute sense to me.

I could not help but wonder, and fear – what was to come 'after', then? Would I remember any of this once I was dismantled and my wooden limbs thrown into piles? Would there only be glimpses of my past as fragments, or fleeting images, or would I remember nothing at all?

I realised there was no point in wondering. The past and the future resided only as moments that led to now, or came from now. I could not spend the next few days living in moments that didn't even exist. Now was all I had. This, and resigning myself to my fate.

Over the next few days I focused on breathing in the warm country air under my eaves. I took in the mountain in all its splendour, the sunset's glowing pink and orange against its blue-tinged rock. I paid attention to the sounds of the night birds calling to one another under a star-filled sky, and I relished the dawn chorus as the sun crept over the paddocks to the East.

I remembered back to when I had first become aware, and my very first occupants, Wattie and his little dog Tess. Then I took the time to picture the face of every one of the people who had lived here, thanking them silently for all they had given me, and taught me, about what it was to 'live'.

I bathed in the warmth of the sunlight hitting my roof, and when a soft afternoon sun-shower came through, I relished the feeling of the water running along the rivulets in my corrugated iron roof.

The next morning, David arrived with Joan and the two of them took some photos of me from the front and back. I felt happy that they wanted to keep some memories of me other than the ones they had made when they lived here.

Then a huge truck with a crane attached to it came and pulled into my driveway, and long thick wires, twisted into something that resembled a cradle, were attached to my base and sides.

As I was lifted slowly onto the back of the truck, I thought about the first time I had been moved here from across the road on a horse and rolling logs! This was certainly going to be an experience, riding on the back of a truck! Despite the fact I was going to an uncertain fate, I almost felt a small thrill at this final, great adventure.

"See how beautiful the house looks!" I heard Joan say to David, above the noise of the crane. "All proud and straight, sitting there on the back of the truck!" They gave one another a wistful, sad look and wrapped their arms around one another.

And slowly, as the truck began to pull away, inching out of the drive and onto the Eltham Road, with all of me balanced atop, Joan and David waved me goodbye.

"Goodbye, House!" they called, smiling and waving their arms furiously like children. But I didn't make any noise in return.

Instead, I took in their happy faces and waving arms and whispered very quietly under my eaves:

"Goodbye! And Thank You!"

Chapter 15

The truck gathered some speed as we moved along the Eltham Road, but it was still slow going.

I noticed now there was a vehicle in front with a flashing light that seemed to be warning other motorists I was coming through.

I couldn't help but feel slightly proud as people slowed their cars, and others came out of their homes to watch me pass.

I was moving Westwards now, towards Opunake, where I knew the wood yard to be.

One moment I felt afraid, but the next I felt exhilarated that this last journey I was taking was one filled with such beauty and wonder.

The fields shone green with summer grasses that would soon be ready for haymaking. Calves skipped and bounced along the fence line as the truck grumbled past. And all the while, the silvery line that defined the ocean's horizon crept closer and closer.

When we turned right at the crossroads and began to head into the town, more people stopped and stared. Children ran alongside the truck, smiling and waving at the driver. Cars cleared both sides of the main street to allow us through. It was my first time of seeing a town, and I was slightly overwhelmed. Look at all the houses, I thought to myself, and all the shops!

I longed to call out to them, to see if they would hear me. Apart from on the television, I had never seen so many people in one place, so many cars, so many colours and words!

And still we drove on, past what looked like a school with a few students gathered at the gate, past tall pine trees surrounding a field of green, where young men dressed all in white chased a little rolling ball into the bushes.

We seemed to be getting to the edge of the town now, and the truck slowed as we negotiated a dip in the road leading out over a bridge. We rounded a corner and were suddenly back out onto the open road. I felt curious and extremely alert now. Where were we going? Perhaps the wood yard was out of town? Perhaps I wasn't going to a wood yard? If not there, then where?

Then I saw it. There to my left, across some fields, I could see the sea! It looked like a blue blanket of shimmering liquid. Now and then white flickers of movement would crest and fall... the waves! I was so caught up in staring at it, I barely noticed where we were going now.

The sea followed us the whole way, staying on my left side, sometimes getting further away as we rounded corners, sometimes coming closer as we approached the coast.

Then we finally began to slow, and a road appeared in front of us that the truck began to turn down. I felt myself shaking… with fear or from the vibrations of the truck, I wasn't even sure, but I did notice the road sign read 'No exit'. The presence of the ocean could no longer distract me. Wherever we were going, this was it for me, I was sure.

I saw a tall white building in the distance that we began to head towards.

The wood yard. It had to be it.

"What's happening? Where are we?!" I wanted to yell. I hated that in this moment I was so terribly alone. If I had been capable, I was sure that this would be when my tears would have fallen. I turned my gaze inwards, not wanting to see, or know, any more.

"Whatever happens now, I just hope it is fast," I said to myself.

Suddenly, the truck slowed and stopped and I heard the whine of the crane as it began to wind out its sinewy cradle.

I heard voices yelling instructions, and felt the wires being affixed to my side and base, and then, the coolness of the air underneath my floor as I began to be hoisted into the sky.

I couldn't take it any longer; I had to see what was happening, and in that moment I suddenly decided what I would do. I would rather rattle myself out of the clutches of this crane and break apart on the ground below than be dismantled by people or shredded by a machine. I readied myself, turned my focus outwards and looked.

I couldn't believe what I saw. At first, I felt shock and disbelief, quickly followed by a series of joyous revelations.

There was the sea. So close I could smell it and hear it. Waves were breaking onto a rocky shore, with a silver band of glittering sand.

All around me were paddocks: beautiful, bright green paddocks, just like in Awatuna.

I could see some other houses to my left, and they were only a few metres away! And the tall white building that I had seen before? We had driven right past it, and now I could see it had a thick black roof, small windows and what looked like a giant lamp on its head.

And there in front of me, as the crane began to lower me towards the ground, were the foundations of what looked to be the footprint of a house. But not just any house – ME!

The joy that filled my insides was overwhelming. I wasn't going to be dismantled! I wasn't going into a wood chipper! I was just being moved!

"Steady, steady!" called a man in a curved yellow hat.

As the crane settled me gently into the foundations, I tried not to quiver with excitement and joy. I wanted to be a perfect fit! I was positioned so that I faced out towards the sea, and the plot was on a slight point.

It was then that I noticed what looked to be a family standing to the right of me, watching as the wires were loosened and disconnected.

There was a man and a woman with their arms around one another, and a little boy of about five clinging onto his father's leg, with the biggest smile on his face. Beside him sat a black and white dog, his pink tongue hanging out of his mouth as he panted in the summer sun.

It was obvious that this was the family that was to live in me, and I felt a surge of happiness.

I saw another, smaller truck laden with black sheets of corrugated iron. A new roof!

There was also a pile of fresh pieces of timber, covered slightly with a sheet of plastic.

Over the next couple of hours, I was attached to my foundations. The truck with the crane reversed out of the gate, and headed off back down the road, and as the sun began to set, the family, and the group of men who had been helping fix me in place, sat down on the piles of the wood, and opened some cans of beer to celebrate.

"Here's to your new house, Alex and Kate!" said one of the men, lifting his can into the air.

"And me and Jinxy!" the little boy called out, raising his plastic cup of juice.

"And you and Jinxy, of course, Bailey darling!" the little boy's Mum, Kate, laughed.

I listened to their conversations, and smiled to myself, already beginning to get to know who my new inhabitants would be.

The sun began to put on a beautiful display, dropping low onto the horizon, filling the sky with a blaze of orange that seemed to light the ocean on fire.

I was absolutely mesmerised by my first ever sunset, especially being so close to the sea.

"See you guys bright and early in the morning, then! Lots of work to do over the next few weeks if we wanna be in by Christmas!" Alex called out to the group of men, as they all climbed into their trucks and cars, and left in convoy out the gate.

When the sun had dropped below the horizon, I kept staring outwards, even as the sky darkened and the first pinpricks of light appeared in the night sky. Clouds began to gather and a cool mist rolled in off the water. The call of birds I had never heard before started up, and the sound of the waves seemed even louder as the darkness crept across the land.

I began to feel myself being lulled into a state of sleep. It had been one of the longest and most emotional days I had ever had, and even though I was excited by the thought of being repaired, perhaps added onto, not to mention a new roof! − I felt exhausted. There would be plenty of time to take it all in when the sun rose in the morning.

As I drifted inwards, it was then that I heard it. Soft at first, like a low whisper, then slightly louder as the voice drifted across on the night breeze.

"And who are you, then?"

I waited and listened. Was that directed at me?

"Don't be shy," said the voice again, "you are among friends." The voice was low and soothing, and seemed to come from the direction of the tall white building.

"Perhaps it doesn't hear us," another voice carried across on the wind. This one higher, and 'younger', maybe?

I daren't believe what I thought I was hearing. These were not the voices of humans. I knew that sound perfectly well. These 'voices' were more like the fluttering of a sheet in the breeze, or the sound the wind used to make in the tall trees across the farm track in Awatuna.

Could it be that these voices were coming from the other houses?

"Who's there?" I whispered back.

There was no reply, and for a moment I thought perhaps I was imagining things.

Then,

"I am Lighthouse," the low, rumbling voice cut through the darkness.

"And I am Red Roof," said the higher voice.

I heard another slightly quieter and raspy voice behind me across the road.

"And I'm Number Four! Welcome."

I was astounded. Through all my years of being surrounded by conversation, moments that I was a part of but could never truly partake in – I had often wondered, even wished, but never for a moment actually believed, that it was possible others like me existed. And yet they did!

"Well?" whispered Lighthouse. "Who are you?"

"I... I am the Little White House." I spoke nervously. I had never given myself a name.

The clouds that had gathered began to disperse and a still white moon spilled its glow over the shore. I could now make out the other houses clearly.

"How… how many of you are there?" I asked. I tried to lift my gaze as far as I could in the darkness, and while I could see some lights through the salt-stunted hedges, I could really only see as far as Lighthouse.

"Well now, including you, there are five of us in total on this side of the boat shed," Number Four replied.

"Five!" I exclaimed, my voice breathless with disbelief and joy. "How amazing!"

"But there are a further four on the other side," Lighthouse informed me. "And, of course, I can see even more across the fields."

"Where did you come from?" Red Roof asked me. "Did you come far?"

I thought about my journey on the back of the truck.

"I came quite far, I think. This is my first time seeing the sea."

The other houses and Lighthouse made 'ahhing' noises, as if nodding their roofs in understanding.

"What… what about you?" I was full of questions, so many questions. How long had everyone been here? What was it like living here? Could the other houses communicate too? But I restrained myself. I felt shy of my new acquaintances.

"I came from New Plymouth, the city," said Red Roof knowingly.

"I came from around the coast," said Number Four. "I was a farm cottage, but since my extension I'm now a proper house!" Number Four's voice was filled with pride and delight.

"And you, Lighthouse?" I asked tentatively. I was a bit intimidated by the tall white building that towered over us.

"I have been here for many, many years," Lighthouse replied in his gentle low tones. "But I was originally put together in another part of the world, before I came here on the back of a ship."

A ship? I was intrigued.

"When I arrived in New Zealand, I was first erected on a small island, and apart from the keeper who manned the light, I was all alone. Then, after ten years or so, I was dismantled again, put on another ship and brought here."

"This was over a hundred years ago, you know!" interrupted Number Four. "Lighthouse, tell the Little White House about the war!"

"The war?" I was gobsmacked now. I didn't know there had ever been a war.

"Oh, yes!" Lighthouse continued, his low voice rising and falling. "There were land wars here between the White Man and the Maori. I even had my own armed constabulary looking after me, such was the vicious battle that raged! But that's a story for another night."

Instead, Lighthouse continued by telling the story of how there had been various keepers looking after the light, until it became automated and, once again, Lighthouse was all alone.

"Alone for a long time, I might add; and though I called out to the houses I could see far across the fields, they never heard me. I wondered if perhaps I was the only one who had a voice. But then one day, a few years ago, Red Roof arrived, and when I spoke…"

"I spoke back!" Red Roof's voice cut through the night air.

"More arrived over the next three years as plots of land here were sold off, and some were built brand new," Lighthouse continued. "Nearly everyone here has come from somewhere else, and everyone has a story to tell."

"And what stories there are!" Number Four whispered delightedly.

"And so, Little White House," Lighthouse asked me, his voice smiling through the darkness, "what is your story?"

"My story?" I paused. I thought back again to all the people who had lived beneath my roof, the things I had seen and experienced, and the emotions I had felt. The music I had heard, the things I had learned; there was so much to tell. There were moments that had brought me joy, and moments that had brought me sorrow. There were things that had made me angry, and things that had made me feel like I was the luckiest house in the world. And now, even when I had thought I was heading to my 'death', I had been given a second chance, in one of the most beautiful locations I could be.

"Well, my story is very long... as I am very old."

"We're all old!" Lighthouse laughed. Not a human laugh, but a deep rumble that mingled and merged with the sound of the waves falling against the sand. "We were all something and somewhere before we became what we are, here in this place, now."

"Well... I wouldn't know where to start," I replied, feeling shy once again.

"I tell you what....," Lighthouse said encouragingly, "why don't you start right back at the beginning?"

And so I began, my voice quavering at first, as I thought back to Jim, the man who had 'made' me, Wattie and Tess, and the night I had nearly been destroyed by fire.

As I went along, my voice often caught as I realised there were certain people I actually felt a deep attachment to, a love, almost, and I realised I could no longer hold back. My roof rattled and my walls heaved as I experienced an outpouring of grief and loss for the first time. I cried out into the night, safe in the knowledge there was no one living within me yet to feel frightened. When I stopped, I felt exhausted, and without speaking any further, I drifted off into a slumberous state, while the others continued to murmur long into the night around me.

I came to know the other houses around me well, and came to know and learn about the people who had lived within their walls. Every story was unique and special, and every one of us listened and questioned and encouraged the others to share.

Over the coming weeks, my limbs were reinforced, and some even replaced. My new roof was strong and shiny, and inside, my rooms were completely renovated with fresh new paint, lush carpet and all modern appliances and furnishings. I had never in my life felt or looked so beautiful or modern.

As for the family who lived within me, they brought me constant joy with their laughter and easy, carefree lives. I watched Alex surf each night after work, only a few metres away from where Kate sat sharing a glass of wine with her neighbour on the new wooden deck that had been added onto my kitchen.

Bailey and Jinx frolicked across the paddocks, playing with other local children, and each evening, when the sky was clear, it was as if the world stopped and watched, as the sunset spread its fiery hands across the sky.

But it was the nights I looked forward to the most now. When the sun had long dropped behind the horizon, and the inhabitants beneath our roofs slept soundly to the beating of the ocean's heart, we houses shared our stories, our thoughts, our dreams. Our voices carried across the fields, soft and quiet, barely audible as more than a whisper on the wind, or the call of a sea bird.

And it was then that I knew, at last, I was more than just a house. I was 'Home'.

AUTHOR'S NOTE

The Little White House is based on the true story of a cottage that was situated on the side of the road in South Taranaki, New Zealand, before being moved to its coastal position where it now resides.

Many of the events that took place within the Little White House are based on actual events and shared recollections.

However, to protect the privacy of those who lived at The Little White House, all names have been changed.

The Little White House as it is now – with its new extension and deck.

The view from the Little White House out to the beach and coastline.

Acknowledgements

I would like to thank my parents Margaret and Ian Scott, who actually lived in the house as a young married couple. Their knowledge of the area and their memories of the house, and all that went on there, helped me greatly in the retelling of the life of The Little White House.

I would also like to thank Brian 'BJ' Smith from Seasons Homestay (www.seasonssurfboards.co.nz) for allowing me to take photos of The Little White House as it is now and giving me permission to use these in this book.

CPSIA information can be obtained
at www.ICGtesting.com
Printed in the USA
LVOW13s2014270318
571329LV00016B/1269/P